ACKNOWLEDGEMENTS

The driving force behind this work has been, from the start, my loving wife Irene, who kept me focused throughout the long and often discouraging process of creation.

Special thanks go to

Martin Elks, PhD for his many hours of dedicated research and editing.

NEBULOUS in Love

A Novel

LeROY CARL BLAKE

Palmetto Publishing Group
Charleston, SC

Nebulous in Love
Copyright © 2019 by LeRoy Carl Blake

All rights reserved
No portion of this book may be reproduced, stored in a retrieval system, or transmitted in any form by any means–electronic, mechanical, photocopy, recording, or other–except for brief quotations in printed reviews, without prior permission of the author.

First Edition

Printed in the United States

Hardcover: 978-1-64111-714-2
Paperback: 978-1-64111-419-6
eBook: 978-1-64111-715-9

TO

Irene Elvin Blake

PRINCIPIUS

Listen! Listen, my friend if you're at your wits' end
    In the nine-to-five race to survive
And you've taken to moping and given up hoping
    That Friday will ever arrive

Come and listen to me as you dodge the debris
    Of the wreck of your wearisome day,
When your world is undone and you cry for someone
    To come peel your puss off the parquet

For I'm bearing a treasure of heart-lifting pleasure
    For all who would wish to partake,
And I'll happily share all the riches I bear
    If my story can keep you awake.

I'm about to unfold a fine fable of old
    (You must listen with all of your might,
For the rhymes that I bring are but words on the wing
    And their magic is found in their flight).

LeRoy Carl Blake

Now, a story well spun is a voyage of fun
      O'er a sea of a whimsical sort,
From the start of our trip in a shimmering ship
      To our happy arrival in port.

And you'll find, as we ride on the outgoing tide,
      That the great *sturm und drang* of your day
Are but ghosts in your mind which we'll leave far behind
      As our bark glides serenely away.

For our journey tonight takes us far out of sight
      To the time of the old Roman Forum,
Where the Rich and the Great met in heated debate –
      Well, they did when they got up a quorum.

We'll sail back to the year sixty-nine which, I fear,
      Seethed with blood-letting hatred and malice,
When new Emperors died with a sword through their hide
      Within weeks upon gaining the palace.

If you're not into hist'ry I'll spare you the myst'ry
      Of who was high man in the steeple:
It was Feckless Despoticus, sovereign eroticus,
      Cherished by all of his people.

NEBULOUS IN LOVE

Now, I've chosen the season, and not without reason:
      The calends of jolly old June.
If we get there much later the heat will be greater,
      And cold if we get there too soon.

Come! Let's pour the martinis! I'll break out the blinis
      And smear them with thick caviar
As our anchor is weighed and our heading is laid
      By the light of yon wandering star.

Then we'll glide o'er the foam on our way to Old Rome
      Where the gods in their Pantheon play;
I will tell you my tale as we run up our sail,
      So, come on then! Let's get under way!

DRAMATIS PERSONAE

Nebulous Ludicrous	A young poet and a nobleman
Virtuous Ludicrous	A Senator; the father of Nebulous Ludicrous
Grievous Vexatious	The leading Senator and most powerful Roman after the Emperor
Pragmaticus Vexatious	The son of Grievous Vexatious and best friend of Nebulous
Ampla Mamaria	The daughter of Grievous Vexatious, twin sister of Pragmaticus, and Nebulous' sweetheart
Phallus Toujourus Erectus	A Praefectus from Milan (Roman Gaul)
Sleazum Emporium	A wine merchant
Flatula Vaporona	The daughter of Sleazum Emporium

LeRoy Carl Blake

Georgeus Gorgeosus	A retired General and powerful Senator, ally of Grievous Vexatious
Hunkus Pectorialus Gorgeosus	The son of Georgeus and an officer in the army
Delicia Gorgeosa	The kid sister of Georgeus Gorgeosus and Pragmaticus' sweetheart
Spectra Hideosa	A widow
Coita Fervida	The younger sister of Spectra Hideosa
Feckless Despoticus	The Emperor
Lascivia Despotica	The wife of the Emperor
Dubius Scrupulous	A General
Renta Pudendum	A Madam

PROLOGUE

Faster! *Faster*, the skilled bearers filled and refilled
    The bright urns that the wine servers bore,
As each server, in turn, filled the cups, from her urn,
    Of the guests who were screaming for more.

Pandemonium reigned! Self-restraint was unchained!
    Bubbling Bacchus kissed everyone's cup;
Even Feckless Despoticus, monarch tosspoticus,
    Had to drink fast to keep up.

For, the Emperor Feckless, that dashing—if reckless—
    Purveyor of bluster and boast,
Was today's honored guest at the beaming behest
    Of one Grievous Vexatious, his host.

In its canny conception this Roman reception,
    So lofty, so lusty, *so lewd*,
Proved that Grievous Vexatious was most efficacious
    In grandly effecting a mood.

LeRoy Carl Blake

Was it not good Vexatious, that wholesome, vivacious
      (And feared) Senate leader, who said:
"Rut and glut without pause while you're living, because
      For a long time you're gonna be dead!"

But the faster the pace meant the faster the race
      Among all of the servants, who bore
The sharp threat of the scourge to encourage their urge
      To forever and always bring *more*.

Wiping sweat from his pate while he quickened their gait,
      Harried Sleazum the wine merchant swore
He'd slash time from the rate of the best rate to date
      At which amphora bearers could pour.

For to Sleazum, the need to improve on the speed
      From clay pot to insatiable lip
Went beyond point of pride, because *saving his hide*
      Could depend on the length of the trip:

"Faster! *Faster,* I say! What's the bloody delay?
      Do you want to be whipped 'til you've bled?
When I cater the wine at a party this fine,
      It's to make me a profit, not *dead*.

NEBULOUS IN LOVE

"We must all persevere, for *the Emperor's here!*
        And a guaranteed, sure way to die
Is to run out of wine – or mescal or moonshine –
        If the living god's cup should run dry.

Having thus made his point, he got bent out of joint
        As he watched while the Emperor drank:
The god knocked back a quart with a sibilant snort,
        And then belched at his heavenly prank.

"I feel pretty damn fine with a belt of that wine,"
        Sweaty Feckless soliloquized. Then,
The Imperial Cup, in an instant filled up,
        Was as instantly empty again.

So, as Feckless, divine connoisseur of fine wine,
        Chased the world drinking record (indoor),
Sleazum knew he'd be dead if he ran out of red
        And more red was not ready to pour.

All his lackeys were bent to their labors, which meant
        He must go by himself, down and back,
By the rear kitchen stair to the wine cellar, where
        Reserve amphorae lay in a rack.

LeRoy Carl Blake

But, as Sleazum descended, his anger transcended
      All thoughts of the present and past,
And he anguished anew, as he often would do,
      On his hopelessly low social caste.

For the merchant, though rich, lacked the *dignitas* which
      Would forever impede his ascent
From the odious mass of the vile merchant class,
      Which was ever his foremost intent.

"Oh, the pain that I bear," Sleazum moaned down the stair,
      "To be richer than these little squirts
And to know beyond doubt I'm forever shut out
      Of their upper-crust clique really *hurts*.

"Freakin' snobs and their brats," mumbled Sleazum. "Those rats
      Treat a wine merchant just like a slave!"
Then the portal he sought interrupted his thought,
      And he pulled on the latch 'til it gave.

But his merchant-class eyes gaped in wanton surprise
      As he opened the huge, oaken door
And beheld, as he froze in a thunderstruck pose,
      What he'd seen in no cellar before:

NEBULOUS IN LOVE

In pink-bottomed profusion and deaf to intrusion
      Two bodies were writhing as one,
So intent on pursuing their common undoing
      That neither knew they'd been undone.

Sleazum couldn't help stare at the passionate pair
      In a mesmerized, dumb sort of shock,
Until deeper reflection – the barest inspection –
      Of facts brought him down like a rock:

A white toga, beneath a fresh laurel-leaf wreath,
      Folded carefully off to the side
Gave the secret away of just who was at play,
      And of why they came down here to hide.

Plus, the arrogant flair— his bum waving in air –
      Made it plain to the dullest acuity
That the man on the floor with his fair paramour
      Must be Grievous, absorbed in fatuity.

But if lovers unclad in the cellar seemed bad,
      The next sight made him wish he had died:
For, the lady down there with her heels in the air
      Was Lascivia, Feckless' young bride.

LeRoy Carl Blake

And – as Sleazum surmised – she was starkly surprised
        To look up and see *him* looking down:
"Who the hell is this jerk with the voyeurist smirk?"
        Purred the wife of the top man in town.

"Jeez! I honestly swear, you can't go anywhere
        Without some little middle-class chump
Getting right in your face – or a more private place –
        With his nose, or his toes, or his rump!"

Sleazum's knees became weak and he barely could speak,
        But he stammered, "Good madam, I fain
Would go some other place and would get there apace
        If to do so would lessen your pain."

But, alas, when he spoke it just served to provoke
        A reaction from Grievous, for whom
The surprise interruption of carnal corruption
        Foreshadowed his possible doom:

"You grape-splattered disgrace to the whole Roman race!
        Does this look like a *spectator sport?*
Get the hell out of here with your lecherous leer,
        Or I'll slit you from starboard to port!"

NEBULOUS IN LOVE

And with that kind rebuff, Grievous, still in a huff,
      Rose with gem-crusted dagger in hand –
As he brought up the knife to cut short Sleazum's life,
      Fair Lascivia said, "Let it stand!

"If you kill him, it's true you'll leave nobody who
      Can bear witness to our little fling;
But if this fool should die feckless' cup will run dry,
      And as host it's *your* neck that he'll wring."

Now then, Grievous, bone bare, his knife still in the air,
      Gave some thought to this roll of the dice;
Then he said in a voice that brooked no other choice,
      "All right, wine merchant, what is your price?"

Having nearly been cooked, Sleazum shook as he looked
      From debaucher to pale debauchee,
But he managed a trace of a smile on his face
      As he whispered, "Why, you can trust *me*.

"Let's not speak of a *price*; won't it surely suffice
      To allow me to call upon you
If the day-to-day strife of my mean, wretched life
      Should require a small favor or two?"

LEROY CARL BLAKE

"He wants favors? From *me*?" Bellowed Grievous as he
    Plumbed Lascivia's naked sang-froid:
"Let me stick the poor slob and be done with the job!
    I can carry the wine for the god."

But the Empress was miffed: "Darling, you couldn't lift
    Even one of the amphorae here;
Besides, what could he ask? Some small, meaningless task
    That your servants could not engineer?

"Anyway, I'm quite sure that this pitiful boor
    Will accept an aureus or two,
So— please cover your loins! – if you'll shell out some coins,
    You'll have given the devil his due."

So, though feeling averse, Grievous reached for his purse
    Full of portraits of Feckless' fat face,
But, on turning around, the wine merchant, he found,
    Had retired without leaving a trace.

"There!" Lascivia said. "The poor booby has fled,
    Out of terror, no doubt, for his hide.
So you see, I was right: He's so frazzled with fright,
    By tonight he'll have curled up and died."

NEBULOUS IN LOVE

Mumbled Grievous, "I doubt we can count the man out.
    See? He even remembered the wine.
Yes, an amphora's gone – *that necessitates brawn* –
    Which, to me, means he's feeling just fine."

After which he expressed, as they hurriedly dressed,
    How he measured their possible fate:
"If the man is a snitch, we'll be axed to death, which
    Has a downside I can't overstate."

"Not to worry, my pet," cooed Lascivia, set
    To return to the party above.
"Wipe the care from your brow as we separate now,
    For that fool lacks the courage whereof

"He would ever approach divine Feckless to broach
    The mean subject of unfaithful wives,
Or to offer that he had espied you and me
    In the closest close-up of our lives."

In a whirl she was gone, and, though Grievous was drawn
    To pursue her, he wisely stayed put:
They must make a clean break for appearances' sake,
    Or risk spelling out what was afoot.

LeRoy Carl Blake

"But of course she is right! We did give him a fright,"
    Chuckled Grievous. "He looked like a ghost!
How could I ever think I'd take heat from that fink?
    . . . Well, I'd better get back and play host."

CHAPTER ONE

Now, the Ludicrous name isn't hoary with fame –
    No, it won't ring a bell in your mind –
But, be that as it may, it was known in its day
    Among Romans as "honor" defined.

In the four hundred years since the Ludicrous peers
    Rose above the mere man in the street,
Honored Ludicrous dead, it was frequently said,
    Were a Who's Who of Roman elite.

But their worth, as it soared, made The Fates become bored
    With the lopsided Ludicrous store
Of good fortune unchecked, beyond theirs to affect,
    So they plotted to even the score.

Thus, the wily Weird Three made this fateful decree –
    They were nothing if not full of fun –
That the Ludicrous presence be pared to its essence
    And bounced back to square number one.

LeRoy Carl Blake

Now, the crux of their plan was reducing the clan
        To *one man* with the Ludicrous name,
Whereupon he alone would advance or dethrone
        Generations of Ludicrous fame.

Thus, the cunning Old Girls, with a toss of their curls,
        Laid a spell on the Ludicrous clan
So the sum procreation of one generation
        Produced only one little man.

But the male interdiction – the one-boy restriction –
        Was only the first of their pearls:
To make sure he was shorn of good luck, he was born
        After ten little Ludicrous girls.

For, the rule of the day to which we've come away
        Was that maids came with cash when they married,
And the dowries they brought were so eagerly sought
        By their grooms that the rule never varied.

Thus, the Ludicrous lands rather quickly changed hands
        To provide for the girls' wherewithal
So their trips down the aisle could be managed in style
        Or, indeed, could be managed at all.

NEBULOUS IN LOVE

The conclusion of which was to happily hitch
      All the girls in the Ludicrous pack,
While their one little man – the sole heir of the clan –
      Remained fiscally flat on his back.

Though he grew to his teens in penurious means
      As if bored to be bothered with gold,
With his Ludicrous stance he stood as straight as a lance
      With his blue-blooded peers, young and old.

Yet, he secretly prized living unsubsidized,
      For this starry-eyed, Ludicrous youth
Was a poet at heart who sought fame through his art
      As a bringer of wisdom and truth.

"What a beautiful day!" We can hear the lad say
      As at noon – the sixth hour – he walked home
With his friend of ten years, from the school of their peers,
      Through the Forum of rowdy old Rome.

"What a morning I've had! All the gods must be mad –
      Or a passable version thereof –
For while you studied Greek and the war of the week,
      I was writing a poem of love."

LeRoy Carl Blake

"Hey, but Nebulous, Greek is the tongue you must speak
      As a Roman Patrician, you know,"
Said his very best friend, "And you'll find, in the end,
      It will pay if you give it a go."

"Ah, Pragmaticus, friend, you will fret 'til the end
      Over language and social position,
But my poems of love tower hugely above
      Aspirations of Roman ambition;

"All of life is a verse and, for better or worse,
      We should welcome it just as it comes,
And not waste it in schools in the charge of old fools
      Learning Greek, Roman conquests, and sums."

And they jostled along through the thick of the throng
      While Pragmaticus offered this thought:
"Well, my mom says the lines of the poets are shrines
      To the concepts their labors have wrought.

"And my sister, of course, likes a real tour de force
      Of the poems of romance and love,
Where the girl gets the guy and together they fly
      To a home in the sky up above;

NEBULOUS IN LOVE

"But my father says rhyme is a pure waste of time
      And the mark of the petty lowborn,
And that they who write verse are a weak-minded curse
      And deserving of better men's scorn."

And as Nebulous' flush tinged the billowing blush
      That Pragmaticus' words had produced,
It emerged like a pox from some Pandora's Box
      Which his friend had unwittingly loosed.

"I am very aware that your pére doesn't share
      Rome's respect for what poets have done,"
Numbly Nebulous sighed, "Though he is, luck aside,
      The most powerful Roman but one;

"And your mother, dear friend, will be blessed to the end
      Of her days with the comforting sound
Of her favorite rhymes, although heard many times,
      With which visions of Heaven abound.

"But alas, only you know the rest of it, too:
      Your twin sister's devotion to art
Has compelled me to write in the hope that I might
      Capture Ampla Mamaria's heart."

LeRoy Carl Blake

Now Pragmaticus knew that in Nebulous' view
      He'd already won Ampla, wherein
He was going to reply, "But you're living a lie!"
      When a fanfare of trumpets broke in.

For, in forging ahead they had threaded their tread
      Through the heart of the heart-beat of Rome,
Where they found they were pressed cheek by jowl with the rest
      Of the world that was calling Rome home.

Now, from out of thin air the sharp trumpeters' blare
      Nearly wakened the dearly departed,
Causing vendors of hats, little boys and stray cats
      To desist from whatever they'd started.

All eyes swiveled around for the source of the sound
      As it echoed from every pilaster,
Quickly focusing *there* at the head of the stair
      To the Temple of Pollux and Castor.

For above the great horde, looking manly and bored,
      A centurion stood with his aide;
And the way he was dressed marked him out from the rest
      Like a king at a beggars' parade.

NEBULOUS IN LOVE

"Awright, lend me your ears and don't give me no sneers!"
      He most boldly began to impart;
"I got somethin' to say and I ain't got all day,
      So close ranks, shut your traps, and look smart."

Winning over the heart of the crowd from the start
      With his charm from the top of the stair,
He continued apace with the same style and grace
      To inform them of why he was there:

"Keep a lid on the talking and olive oil hawking,
      And gather in close to find out
Why I'm standing up here in my Sunday-best gear,
      'Cause I'm damned if you'll force me to shout.

"Um, where was I? Oh, yes: We are flushed with success!
      We're the Mediterranean champs!
And outside them there walls, past the markets and stalls,
      Gen'ral Dubius Scrupulous camps.

"Now the Gen'ral, you know, is a right kind of Joe,
      Who's just marched us all homeward victorious,
With the loot that we brought from the battles we fought
      To the Triumph intended to glory us.

LeRoy Carl Blake

"The campaigns that we waged never could have been staged
      By a leader of any less cunning;
We met every contender of masculine gender
      And sent every man of them running.

"So – his name be respected! – His highness selected
      The day after next to review
The Triumphal Parade of the conquests we made,
      And give Dubius all that he's due.

"Then the games will commence at the Gen'ral's expense
      For a month from the day we begin,
Which I think you'll agree is a hell of a fee
      Just to show the tax bracket you're in."

Then the crowd leaped for joy and began to deploy
      Festive colors at everyone's door
As the news flew like fire through a balsa wood pyre
      That a Triumphal bash was in store.

Within minutes the crowd went from screaming out loud
      To up-raising closed fists in assent,
As the word settled in through the wall-to-wall din
      What the soldier's announcement had meant.

NEBULOUS IN LOVE

"Do you know what that means?" Yelled Pragmaticus, scenes
    Of wild revelry filling his eyes.
"There's a hero out there who's killed more than his share,
    Whom we're going to legitimatize."

"Hey now, that isn't bad!" Rejoiced Nebulous, glad
    That the fête was as good as begun.
"I can sit holding hands in the uppermost stands
    With your sister and watch all the fun."

"Nebulous, Give it up! You behave like a pup
    With your dreams and your poetry, too;
She is out of your reach, for though Pater's a peach,
    His ambitions do *not* include *you*.

"For his number one plan in the Senate, my man,
    Is to foster the Emperor's will,
While he fills up his coffers with scandalous offers
    And kickbacks for passing each bill.

"And with that set of views it would hardly be news
    That my sister is destined to climb
To much loftier stations than close-knit relations
    With Nebulous, writer-of-rhyme."

LeRoy Carl Blake

Thus, with guilt mixed with pride, young Pragmaticus tried
    To make Nebulous' heart understand.
"The requirements to marry my sister don't vary:
    They're money, position, and land."

"But it's *love* that I send her each day that I tender
    A poem drawn straight from my heart;
Can't your dad understand how I yearn for her hand
    After Cupid let fly with his dart?"

"Look, I'm not a romantic – just sort of pedantic –
    So listen and stop parvenu-ing:
Though my sister digs Cupid she'd have to be stupid
    To tell dear old Dad what you're doing.

"You're a poet at heart, and that's great, for a start.
    And, I know Ampla thinks you're the tops.
But if you're making plans to go posting the banns,
    You're about to get knocked off your props.

"For, although your blood's blue, for my dad that won't do
    'Cause you're flat on your financial tush;
What you lack is the land (That's a bird in the hand)
    And the prospects (that's one in the bush).

NEBULOUS IN LOVE

"Which all means, my good friend, it's no good to pretend
    That dear Pater would ever allow
Any man to propose to his fresh, budding rose
    If that man isn't gold-plated *now*."

And, with that statement made, the boys' two-man parade
    Elbowed through to the Palatine Stair,
Which they climbed to the top before making a stop
    At the door of the grandest house there.

"Though a trifle ornate, here's your humble front gate,"
    Mumbled Nebulous, kiddingly callous;
"But, I shouldn't berate the Vexatious estate:
    Be it ever so poor, it's a palace."

"Yeah, the house is okay in a vast kind of way,"
    Said Pragmaticus, turning to leave,
"If you're into impressing the neighbors or stressing
    What money and clout can achieve.

"But for my simple taste it's all just a big waste;
    It's a villa with too many rooms,
Filled with statues and things that preeminence brings
    But they all feel like cold, lonely tombs."

LeRoy Carl Blake

"Yes, I'm sure that they do," agreed Nebulous, who
      Was now handing a scroll to his friend.
"Please give this to your sister and tell her I've missed her,
      And mind all the hugs at the end."

"Sure, consider it sent," sighed Pragmaticus, bent
      Upon being a friend to his friend,
Even though in his heart he was sure from the start
      It would do him no good in the end.

Now the daily routine had, for Nebulous, been
      To walk on to his own habitation,
Where Calliope breathed, with her sisters, the wreathed
      Evanescence of bold inspiration.

But today a surprise was to greet the boys' eyes
      That the lads could in no wise ignore:
Today Grievous Vexatious, the father of gracious
      Pragmaticus, stepped from his door.

And the man, as he strode from his gate to the road,
      Was engaged in the spirited telling
Of a secret held dear, which the boys couldn't hear,
      To a man who was grossly repelling:

NEBULOUS IN LOVE

". . . And, although it's audacious," growled Grievous Vexatious,
      "No fetters bind Sleazum's ambition:
The fool now expects *me* to do everything *he*
      Thinks will heighten his social position.

"And, should I fail to do what he orders me to,
      From the stench of his wine dealer's dive,
He has sworn he will steer to the Emperor's ear
      A slight 'rumor' which I won't survive."

Now he whispered, "It's true! And I'm just telling you
      Because you've known me all of my life
That the wine merchant saw me get down in the straw
      With Lascivia, Feckless' young wife.

"Because Sleaze, you'll recall, supplied wine for the ball
      Which I laid on for Feckless last week,
And could now testify he was watching while I
      Showed the lady my Latin technique."

His repellent companion – as big as a canyon –
      Pulled back in amazement and said,
"With the wife of the *god?* How incredibly odd
      That he hasn't yet lopped off your head!"

LeRoy Carl Blake

"But of course *that's the point!*" Grievous croaked, out of joint
    That his friend hadn't yet understood,
"If I don't do his bidding, he's really not kidding—
    My wife would just *hate* widowhood!

"But the worst was this morning. It came without warning,
    When I was compelled to invite
By command, read aloud, the complete Senate crowd
    To an orgy he's throwing tonight.

"Well, his party tonight has me really uptight;
    I'm becoming a quivering wreck!
But if I don't attend I'm afraid I will end
    With no head and a very short neck."

As this whisper was shared young Pragmaticus stared,
    And he gasped, "May Minerva protect us!
The fat Celt with my dad is a blue-blooded cad,
    Namely Phallus Toujourus Erectus."

The boys froze where they stood – as if hewn out of wood –
    Because now they could hear what was said:
". . . And this orgy tonight twists my gut up in fright:
    If the Sleaze breathes a word I'll be *dead*."

NEBULOUS IN LOVE

Grievous then saw the pair, of whom one was his heir,
      And he spun where he stood in the street
And to Nebulous said, "Stick *this* rhyme in your head:
      Leave my daughter alone *tout de suite!*

"Every poem I've found to my daughter is bound
      For the flames of the trash pit *today,*
So don't waste further scrolls turning words into coals
      In your boyish attempt to make hay!"

He then scathingly read from a poem he said
      Was mere juvenile lewdness withal,
Though while standing quite near he contrived not to hear
      Heavy breathing that came from the Gaul.

Calmly, Nebulous said as the statesman turned red,
      His eyes smoldering dark and predacious,
"I'm so glad you're well-read!" Then, he bolted and fled
      As the Celt took his rhymes from Vexatious.

And he ran as if Youth could outrun Naked Truth
      In its innocent quest to survive,
And careened through the gate of his father's estate
      Giving thanks that he made it alive.

LeRoy Carl Blake

But, down deep in his heart he was pained that his art
    Had been used to debase and disparage
By the father of she whom he'd reckoned would be
    The fair bride at his hoped-to-be marriage.

But he couldn't have guessed, as his feet came to rest,
    That his rhymes were now held by that *toad*
Who had taken control of each long, loving scroll
    From Vexatious back there in the road.

CHAPTER TWO

Though once nestled among all the smugly top rung
    Roman homes of the richly ordained,
The old Ludicrous place – paradigm of pure grace –
    Was now one of the few that remained.

For, as hist'ry recounts, to acquire the amounts
    (*How it seemed to be just yesterday!*)
Of the land he would need Nero burned, in his greed,
    Every building that stood in his way.

Nero's palace, in fact, had usurped every tract
    From the Palatine Hill, which it topped,
Through the ravaged defile for just over a mile
    To the Esquiline Hill, where it stopped.

Though not *all* the conjoined bits of land were purloined
    From the cream of the Roman elite,
Nero's palace just spanned the best part of the land
    On the Palatine save for one street.

LeRoy Carl Blake

And it's this lonely road that Our Hero's abode
      Was so handsomely given to grace,
At the opposite end from the steps that descend
      From Vexatious' luxurious place.

But, no matter the years it had stood among peers
      In the glory that once was its due,
The old Ludicrous place was today a disgrace
      Of bare walls and a throw rug or two

Wherein great, brooding spaces paid homage to places
      Silk couches had once been enjoyed,
And where objects of gold, piece-by-piece long since sold,
      On great tables had once been deployed.

Every gray little room was a haven of gloom,
      Standing quiet for year upon year,
And young Nebulous swore as he slammed the great door
      That disaster was chillingly near.

Without stopping he raced from the doorway in haste,
      Making straight for his cubicle, where
Every day he made camp with a desk and a lamp
      And the foot of his bed for a chair.

NEBULOUS IN LOVE

The bright lunchtime in June became mid-afternoon
    As the boy-poet pondered his fate:
Until midday today the whole world went my way –
    Why did everything change on this date?

All he'd asked from Above was the hand of his love
    And the gift from the Muse to ensure
That his poems command universal demand
    And, of course, that his fame would endure.

Was it asking too much for an artist of such
    Modest temper and flawless humility
To be honored by all from Phoenicia to Gaul,
    Heaping praise on his massive ability?

Although sick in his heart he returned to his art,
    And he swiftly picked up on the thread
Of the verse he'd been hatching for weeks without scratching
    The surface of dreams in his head.

He poured forth about love, and of Heaven above,
    And of fights to the very last breath,
And of mortals at odds with mercurial gods
    And of triumphs and taxes and death.

LeRoy Carl Blake

And he wrote about life, and of Jupiter's wife,
    And the duel 'twixt wrongness and right,
And was writing still more when a knock at the door
    Put Erato and Thalia to flight.

Brave Calliope stuck, full of mythical pluck,
    Just to see who was causing the bother,
But she, too, took the air when it opened, and there
    Appeared Virtuous, Nebulous' father.

"Welcome home," the lad said without turning his head.
    "Are you playing the truant from town?
Your sedate, lordly face doesn't normally grace
    Home and hearth 'til the sun has gone down."

"Yes, I know," the man said, "But I fear I am fed
    To the teeth with the Forum these days,
With some Senators yelling and others foretelling
    Our doom if we don't mend our ways,

"And I missed all the bold, great debaters of old
    In today's petty, boorish dispute,
So I slipped through the ranks of those Curia cranks,
    And walked home by the grain market route."

NEBULOUS IN LOVE

Something, Nebulous thought, made his father distraught,
    For no legions, in ten million years
Could drive Virtuous home from the Senate of Rome
    In the midst of a row with his peers;

For, though Virtuous, just a back-bencher, was thrust
    To the side in important debates,
He had won their salute as the man most astute
    In the Senate's most holy estates

Which were: Honor, to wit: His high principles fit
    Unimpeachable ethics of yore,
When the Senate was billed as an institute filled
    With inviolate virtues galore;

And Integrity, which, with a character rich
    In the standards of what's right and wrong,
Meant, as everyone knew – and his record speaks true –
    He was genuine, thorough, and strong.

"It's not like you at all to walk out on a brawl
    And show up here in daylight like this,"
Observed Nebulous then as he laid down his pen,
    "And I'd like to know what's gone amiss."

LeRoy Carl Blake

Several minutes went by without any reply
    Before Virtuous finally said,
"What has 'gone quite amiss' is, we've reached the abyss,
    And the precipice lies dead ahead.

"After four hundred years with our spotless careers,
    And the Senate's most prized reputation,
You're the last-conceived man of the Ludicrous clan,
    And we now face complete ruination.

"For what good has it done to become Number One
    If we've naught for our own livelihood,
And no servant to hie to the market to buy
    What we can't, even granting we could?

"No, in truth I returned to this house roundly spurned
    By the venal, rich Senators who
Run the place like a club and summarily snub
    Those of us who aren't millionaires too.

"But the tragedy lies not in their greedy eyes,
    But that when your belov'd mother died,
With my youth, charm, and grace and this Ludicrous face,
    I could surely have found a new bride.

NEBULOUS IN LOVE

"But I just couldn't act for the plain, simple fact
    That her memory stayed in my heart,
And I had no desire to extinguish that fire,
    So I never did make a new start.

"But I should have, of course, and now, filled with remorse,
    I am sorry that I never wed
A rich widow, relieved of her husband, bereaved
    On becoming conveniently dead."

"But your love was so real, I know just how you feel,"
    Answered Nebulous, "And I agree!
For, to make lovers whole requires soul meeting soul,
    Which is what every marriage should be."

Softly, Virtuous said, slowly shaking his head,
    "No, I made a mistake, I now know,
For while love gives you chills, it won't spare you from bills
    Or from being chucked out in the snow;

"Nor will love buy the deed to the land you will need
    To get into the Senate one day,
For each new man of rank must have cash in the bank
    Or the Senate will turn him away.

LeRoy Carl Blake

"But, be that as it may, I've come home, as I say,
      To get out of that snobby-nosed mob,
And to tell you it's time to stop fooling with rhyme
      And make marriage your number one job."

But when Nebulous' eyes tilted up toward the skies,
      As he silently sat on the bed,
The old Senator knew he was not getting through,
      So he waited a moment, and said:

"Ah, my son, why remain in this dismal domain?
      You've turned day into coldhearted night.
Must you hide in the gloom of this shadowy room
      While you think up more poems to write?"

But the boy, steely-eyed and unmoving, replied,
      "I'm so glad you came early today;
You don't normally start to unload on my art
      Until supper has been cleared away."

"Mind your manners, young man! I'm still head of this clan,
      And, though maybe I'm short in the purse,
At least I spend my days in Rome's service in ways
      That exceed writing frivolous verse."

NEBULOUS IN LOVE

Quickly, Nebulous said as he leaped from the bed
      And laid hold of the light-giving lamp,
"You are right, Pater dear, it *is* gloomy in here.
      I will take your advice and decamp."

But the Senator's glare at his arrogant heir
      Halted Nebulous cold in his tracks;
The man counted to ten before speaking again,
      And then whispered, "Why don't you relax?

"Your eternal affront at my urgent – if blunt –
      Warning shots that you're wasting your time,
Not to mention disdain for all those who remain
      Disinclined to go mad for your rhyme,

"Is beginning to wear just a tiny bit bare
      And I think it is time in your life
You stopped jerking around and got out there and found
      A rich widow to take for a wife."

"A rich *what?*" gasped the lad as the bolt from his dad
      Struck him hard, like a kick to the groin,
"You want *me* to belong to some witch who's as long
      In the tooth as she is in the coin?

LeRoy Carl Blake

"By the gods up above, don't you know that true love
      Is the only real justification
That good conscience allows for exchanging those vows –
      Not endowments and cash compensation!

"And besides (after all, if you'd care to recall),
      I have already chosen a mate
To whom I shall be wed, as I often have said,
      On my poems' first publishing date."

Sadly, Virtuous sighed, holding so much inside
      That he couldn't explain to his son,
Like the time it would take for a poet's first break,
      Never mind being equaled by none;

Or that poets earned less than the price of a dress,
      Which a wife has been known to resent,
Or, the worst of the worst, which he'd have to face first,
      Which was Grievous' cold lack of consent.

For the arrogant lord of Vexatious' great hoard
      Wouldn't ever consider a plan
For his daughter to wed the sole heir of the head
      Of the ill-favored Ludicrous clan.

NEBULOUS IN LOVE

"You love lyrical art, and your mother, dear heart,
      Had a love for great poetry, too,
And it must have been she (Well, it sure wasn't me!)
      Who bequeathed all your talent to you.

"For your mother *was* love, like a velvety glove
      Smoothing over the cares of the day,
And if she hadn't died, she'd be here at my side
      Knowing just what to do and to say.

"But the problem, you see, is you're stuck with just me,
      And a future, I fear, just as bleak,
Unless you can persuade a rich widow to trade
      Her estate for your blood's bluish streak."

"But," young Nebulous said, "The whole issue is dead,
      As I've told you so often before.
Why can't anyone see that I've got to be me
      In this world full of rules I deplore?"

"My young son, try to see what it's like to be *me*
      In a world in which none hold the rein
To the galloping horse we call destiny's force,
      Or to anything else, in the main;

LeRoy Carl Blake

"Where pathetically few live a life with a view
    From the top of the Palatine Hill,
And the number of teens who get by without means
    Is a hell of lot fewer still.

"I am stuck in this state because all of my late
    Happy brothers and cousins had girls,
Most of whom, as they swung down the aisle were so young
    They had barely outgrown baby curls;

"And the dowry we paid for each misty-eyed maid
    To be happily wooed, won, and wed,
Left the Ludicrous purse all the more for the worse,
    And our worth, in the end, in the red.

"So, when all's said and done, we are back to square one:
    We're in debt, we've no land, and we're broke;
That leaves you, Buckaroo, to go out and come through
    With a wife with a pile in her poke."

By the lamp's ruddy glow the young man stood to go,
    Letting Virtuous know he was vexed;
And in straightforward prose he said, "Pater, who knows
    What demands you will make on me next!

NEBULOUS IN LOVE

"From the time I was small the one thing I recall
      About you, besides daring and dash,
Was your promise to me I would always be free
      To get married for love and not cash;

"Well, it seems pretty clear that if we're inching near
      To the edge of calamity now,
That perhaps it is *you* w*h*o should start pitching woo
      To whomever will give you her vow."

"Don't get carried away by the passionate play
      Of romance that belabors your rhyme;
If you think, you'll concur that all women prefer
      A young stud in the heat of his prime."

"How can you be so sure?" Queried Nebulous. "You're
      Not exactly out shaking the bushes.
Look around. You'll find *lots* of old ladies with hots
      For you older guys' blue-blooded tushes."

"My, you do have a way with the things that you say,"
      Countered Virtuous, trying his best
Not to laugh at the thought of his toga pulled taut
      While his buttocks were duly assessed.

"But, in truth we both know it's no longer my show;
 Now the torch has been passed on to you.
You are at center stage, where young men of your age
 Have the 'tushes' that women pursue."

"But I'm sure you know *one*," said the Senator's son
 With the hint of a mischievous smile,
"Who's got coffers of gold filled with all they can hold
 And been widowed a very long while,

"And of whom we have heard no disparaging word,
 And *from* whom there have been no complaints,
And who surely would move toward a chance to improve
 On her middle class social constraints."

But his father insisted no woman existed
 In Rome with that specification:
"Be assured I would know of a wonderment so
 Made to measure for my situation."

"But you do," said the lad, who now laughed as his dad
 Racked his brain to unriddle the name;
"Hideosa is who I'm referring you to:
 She's one awesomely affluent dame."

NEBULOUS IN LOVE

Stately Virtuous paled upon being assailed
      By that name, like a slap on the cheek:
"Must you make manifest manly fears in your jest?"
      He exclaimed when at last he could speak.

"Hideosa, my son, was a fountain of fun
      When her husband was there at her side,
But once left all alone she became an old crone,
      All because her beloved had died.

"For to tell you the truth, in the days of her youth
      Before rage at her fate took its toll,
She was all charm and grace, with a beautiful face,
      And was really quite witty and droll.

"But alas, it is true that as time passed she grew
      More contentious and bitterness-prone,
Till in ripe middle age, though she's spent all her rage,
      Still her face remains hard as a stone."

"And I seem to recall – back when I was just small" –
      Put in Nebulous, "Though it was brash,
How we joked even then what a man among men
      It would take to touch *that* lady's stash."

LeRoy Carl Blake

"Yes, and we weren't alone. Every nobleman's moan
    When indebtedness led him to strife
Was, 'If things don't improve I have one final move:
    I can take Hideosa to wife.'"

"But then," Nebulous said, since she never re-wed,
    It is simple enough to infer:
She's so hard on the eyes that those desperate guys
    Faced their creditors rather than her."

"All of which, good or bad, leads to nothing, my lad,
    For we're still at the place we began:
We've a larder that's bare and no money to spare,
    And you've still not agreed to my plan.

"It is not for old men to get married again,
    But for youth on its march to the fore –
For the sake of our home and the future of Rome,
    Will you *please* think it over once more?"

Once again, in the quiet, his reason ran riot
    As Nebulous fought with his soul;
And his soul won the day, for he heard himself say,
    "I'm afraid I cannot play that role.

NEBULOUS IN LOVE

"I will marry for love, as the heavens above
      Are my witness to all that I've said,
And I swear to you now that if I break this vow,
      May the witnessing gods strike me dead!"

Conquered, Virtuous stood as a true Roman should,
      And he waved toward the rhymes on the bed:
"You must put away these and change quickly now, please,
      For an orgy at Sleazum's," he said.

"The *wine merchant?* It's odd that he'd give you the nod
      To go romp at his villa tonight;
You buy nothing at all from his rank little stall
      Which is less of a stall than a blight!"

"I was given no choice," sighed his father's tired voice.
      "You know I have no truck with the masses,
But Vexatious, today, for what cause I can't say,
      Has committed all Rome's upper classes."

"*Aha!*" Nebulous, bugged by a memory, tugged
      At the thread of a comment he'd heard,
When Vexatious had said to the Celt, "*I am dead*
      If the merchant breathes even a word."

LeROY CARL BLAKE

"It would seem," mused the boy, "That this unabashed ploy
    Means that Grievous has something to hide,
And that Sleazum knows what, and will keep his mouth shut
    In exchange for a guaranteed ride

"To the upper crust plain of Rome's social terrain
    And away from the wine peddlers' stalls;
And tonight, maybe I will discover just why
    Grievous jumps when Emporium calls."

But the man standing there couldn't possibly care
    Any less about who jumped for whom;
Unequivocally spurned, the old Senator turned
    And walked out of the small, dingy room.

In the atrium's light as the shadows of night
    Wrapped the big, empty villa in shade,
Grumbling Virtuous talked to himself, as he walked,
    Of the son he had failed to persuade.

In his own private cloud, he reflected aloud:
    "Why couldn't I be the sire of a winner!"
Feeling left in the lurch, he kept walking in search
    Of some morsel to have for his dinner.

CHAPTER THREE

Though the night was still young and the sky barely hung
    With a spatter of stars now and then,
The near deafening level of hot-blooded revel
    Meant Sleazum's to-do was a ten.

The wine flowed like the Tiber and every imbiber
    Pursued his or her carnal credo,
Though the noise of the crowd was so god-awful loud
    One could hardly hear one's own libido.

"This immense peristyle makes our Ludicrous pile
    Look like Ceres' old gardening shed,"
Hollered Virtuous, vying with those who were trying
    To talk and to hear what was said;

"The *real* orgy, I'm told, where young maidens make bold
    To feed grapes to their dates in the buff,
Is beyond yonder wall in the atrium hall,
    Which tonight hardly seems big enough."

LeRoy Carl Blake

Walking on side by side, son and father both tried
    To appear to be hip to the core,
But their eyes fairly popped when the two of them stopped
    To look in at the atrium door:

Those whose togas weren't off were preparing to doff
    As constraints on propriety waned:
All the topers were groping while gropers were hoping
    To rip off what raiment remained.

What a wonderful ball! In attendance were all
    But the Emperor and his brigadesmen,
For not even Vexatious with threats imprecatious
    Could lure him to dine with a tradesman.

Turning back on their heels from the giggles and squeals
    To a scene that was far less salacious,
They kept off to the side of the on-rushing tide
    And wound up behind . . . Grievous Vexatious!

Quickly Nebulous said, "Father, please go ahead –
    I will follow on closely behind;
By this means one will spot what the other does not,
    And then later we'll share what we find."

NEBULOUS IN LOVE

So, like brackets, the pair tailed Vexatious to where,
      In a corner away from the mob,
In a close tete-a-tete the great Senator met
      With their host, the proud wannabe snob.

Slowly, Virtuous inched toward the two who were clinched
      In a mutual verbal assault,
Till he got in position to hear with precision
      How each called the other to fault.

But just then, in tableau, he saw Nebulous glow
      At the sight of his girl and her brother,
Where the love of his heart and his pal stood apart
      With their elegant, richly-robed mother.

Ampla's eyes spoke of love, and of pleasures above
      All his wildest, impossible yearning;
Though he didn't dare speak, the boy's knees became weak,
      And down south all his bridges were burning.

With his son in a daze under Ampla's fond gaze,
      Hapless Virtuous sighed, "I give up!"
And returned his attention to those in contention
      As serving girls topped up his cup.

Leroy Carl Blake

"Now you look!" Grievous glared at the merchant, who dared
        To aspire to a new social height,
"As you crassly demanded, I rankly commanded
        These blue-bloods to be here tonight.

"Every man of them's rich, and of ancestry which
        Should provide the prestige you so covet,
And they came to this show with their families in tow,
        So if that's not enough, you can shove it!"

"Touchy, *touchy*," Sleaze said with a shake of his head,
        "Our good friendship is worth more than talk;
All you've done, Mr. Smarty, is come to a party.
        Is that any reason to squawk?"

Then the Senator said, turning very deep red,
        "What *good friendship*, you towering twit!
If you think I extend the firm hand of a friend,
        You've a widget in place of a wit."

"Oh, come, *come* now, dear *friend*, surely you don't intend
        For this orgy tonight to be all
That we share with each other – may I call you 'Brother?' –
        Oh my, I'm just having a ball!"

NEBULOUS IN LOVE

But on being so goaded Vexatious exploded:
    "I shouldn't have left you alive!
For I see I shall pay through the nose every day
    For as long as I manage to thrive;

"What in hell would there be you could offer to me
    That I'd want from a peasant like you?
As well-heeled as you are, I've more riches by far,
    And the blood in *my* veins is pure blue!"

"Why, Vexatious, dear *friend,* wherefore seek to offend?
    Now, you already know our accord:
Just provide what I ask, and for each finished task
    Golden silence shall be your reward."

Grievous' ears fairly smoked, and his throat was so choked
    That his voice became raw and unsure,
But he managed to rasp in a gravelly gasp,
    "How much more of this must I endure?"

"There, there, *there,* my old *friend,* we've not come to the end
    Of the wonderful things we can share;
I've a lovely surprise for your upper crust eyes,
    And she's standing behind you, just there."

LeRoy Carl Blake

Sleazum held forth his hand in a silent command
    Toward his object of fatherly pride:
She wore long, greasy hair and had pimples to spare,
    And an aura no perfume could hide.

"My *friend* Grievous, I pray, step a little this way;
    There is someone I'd like you to meet:
My fair daughter – my Honey – who'll inherit my money:
    She's Flatula. Isn't she sweet?"

Now the Senator, cool under fire and no fool,
    Couldn't fathom why he'd been presented
To this frightful young creature, so void of fair feature,
    And more than just troublingly scented.

So, the merchant spelled out, lest there be any doubt,
    What the price of his silence would carry:
"To reward my discretion *In re:* Your transgression,
    Your son and my daughter shall marry."

Grievous staggered in shock as he felt the room rock,
    And his face in sheer horror was frozen,
While the merchant escorted his daughter, transported
    By love to the husband he'd chosen.

NEBULOUS IN LOVE

And Pragmaticus, too, stung by Sleazum's bold coup,
      Felt the merchant's hot words in his face:
"Your old man is okay, but to keep him that way
      This here marriage had better take place!"

For poor, humbled Vexatious, the great, disputatious
      Purveyor of truth in the land,
Never ever looked worse, or more sad, or perverse,
      Any hour than the hour now at hand.

In the shreds of his pride and no place he could hide
      From the air of that odious daughter,
He was wracked with despair that his sole son and heir
      Would be sent by the Sleaze to the slaughter.

Then, in Grievous' deep gloom, from the huge, crowded room
      Billowed forth an imposing Praefectus;
Like the hope of dawn's light in the pit of the night,
      It was . . . Phallus Toujourus Erectus!

The Celt oozed to a stand near the quivering hand
      Of Vexatious (resigned to his fate),
And said, "I'll put this right! Get your son out of sight
      While I find Eau de Merde a new mate."

Leroy Carl Blake

With which, braving the essence of Flatula's presence,
    He whispered, "My dear, you're sublime.
It's your charm and your flair (not to mention your air)."
    Then he slipped her young Nebulous' rhyme.

And as Flatula read, words of love filled her head
    While the Celt murmured ever so sweetly,
"That was written for you by a young noble who
    Is insane for your love – well, discreetly."

Gently prying her fist from Pragmaticus' wrist
    Before wrenching her smoothly away,
Phallus wrestled the brat to where Nebulous sat,
    And he whispered, "This must be your day."

"Did you write this for me? I'm so thrilled I could pee!"
    Greeted Nebulous' ears, and he started;
But what greeted his eyes was much more the surprise,
    And what greeted his nose roundly smarted.

"Gee, I'm terribly sorry. You've bagged the wrong quarry,"
    Young Nebulous tried to explain,
But she bellowed with zest, *"Merde ardua est!"*
    As she sent forth an air of disdain.

NEBULOUS IN LOVE

With that token of grace firmly slammed into place,
    She dived into the atrium's roar,
Hauling Nebulous in to the rollicking din,
    Leaving Virtuous, shocked, at the door.

And the wine merchant, who, had been blindsided too,
    Wondered how he had taken the hit;
While his eyes were on Phallus O *bringer of malice!*
    Vexatious and family had split.

CHAPTER FOUR

The first stars of the night, having wound out of sight
    As the sky turned relentlessly west,
Were replaced by the light of the moon in its flight
    As it followed its own westward quest.

At Emporium's ball things had slowed not at all
    As the moon, like the stars, sought the crest
Of the hills west of Rome that the sunset calls home,
    And where darkness, at dawn, goes to rest.

And in one of the rooms, full of buckets and brooms
    And as small as a pinchpenny's tip,
Trembling Nebulous slouched where he'd spent the night crouched
    After slipping poor Flatula's grip.

Since the moment he'd run from The Redolent One
    When she paused long enough to assess
An equestrian force (A guy hung like a horse)
    He kept hearing her voice screaming, "Yesss!"

NEBULOUS IN LOVE

Now he sighed with delight: "I could hide here all night!
    But that isn't the truth and I know it;
She's still out there somewhere in her rarified air
    Searching upstairs and down for her poet."

He ripped open the door on the rollicking roar
    Of the free-loving mob still assembled,
And was gladdened to see as he set himself free
    From the mops that he no longer trembled.

In this much improved state he made straight for the gate
    Past a dozen high columns or two,
When he suddenly found he could hear every sound
    From behind them, of voices he knew:

"Oh-ho! Phallus, I see you're as low-down as me!"
    It was Grievous, who couldn't help beaming.
"Your finesse was so cool that that wine merchant fool
    Never knew he was getting a reaming."

"Well, now, what are friends for?" Glowed the adipose bore
    As he warmed to Vexatious' ovation;
"Any friend would have done what I did for your son,
    In the name of a friend's obligation."

LeRoy Carl Blake

"But you *acted*, my friend! That's what counts in the end.
    Why, unflinching, you joined in the fight!
And while Sleazum, right now, may be having a cow,
    We at least dodged the trident tonight.

"And what's more, mon ami," laughed Vexatious with glee,
    Heaping praises on Phallus Erectus,
"Make a wish, if you will, for my pleasure to fill
    As my thanks that you never neglect us."

"Ah, largesse," cooed the Celt, "Is a word I have felt
    Was invented especially for you:
You've a fortune as great As a Near Eastern state,
    Yet you want to give me something, too.

"I am humbled indeed that you've chosen to heed
    A mere act of my friendship so slight
That I paid it no mind, beyond just being kind,
    When I rescued your buttocks tonight."

"And that just goes to show," beamed Vexatious, aglow
    At the center of all the attention,
"Your deeds *can't* be dismissed, which is why I insist:
    You may have anything you can mention."

NEBULOUS IN LOVE

Phallus buried his guile as the hint of a smile
      Twinkled first in one eye and then both;
Then he took heart to say, "I will have, if I may,
      The fair hand of your daughter in troth."

"Why, you miserable snail! You ... you ...lowborn *canaille!*
      You'd presume to have dreams of my daughter?
Why, your brain is as flat as your belly is fat
      If you think this cheap trick will have bought her!

"With your black reputation throughout all Creation
      For ravishing maidens you savor,
Did you think that this ram would hand over his lamb
      To the wolf for a piddling *favor?*

"Well, stick this in your laurels, you hick without morals!
      You rotund, barbaric factotum!
You stay out of my way, or I'll see that you pay
      In the coin of your overtaxed scrotum!"

And with that, having spurned the one man who had earned
      His respect (not to mention his praise),
The Great Man spun about and strode haughtily out,
      Leaving Phallus behind in a daze.

LeROY CARL BLAKE

It took less than a second, the Praefectus reckoned,
      To kill what he'd nurtured for years,
But their friendship was *dead,* and as Grievous now fled
      The Celt's eyes overran with hot tears.

But, although he was stung by the tone of the tongue
      That rained blows on his Gallic esteem,
It made only a dent in his cavalier bent
      And his mind began hatching a scheme:

"I'll take none of your sass, you imperious ass!"
      He let fly in the solon's direction;
"Oh, revenge will be good when the pure maidenhood
      Of your daughter augments my collection!"

Now, Young Nebulous knew, though still hidden from view,
      What had passed between Roman and Celt,
And he understood, too, what the Celt planned to do
      To make up for the snub that he felt.

Oh, ye gods! Was it true? What was he going to do?
      Phallus planned to deflower his girl!
And he swore then and there *By all gods* he would spare
      His true love from that scurrilous churl.

NEBULOUS IN LOVE

His heart heavy with gloom, he turned back toward the room
    And saw Virtuous, doing his duties
As the center-most part of a three-layered tart
    'Twixt a couple of ravishing beauties.

He cried, "Father! I'm here!" jarring Virtuous clear,
    Which threw everyone into confusion.
"Oh, it's you," his dad said. "Gee, my endless search led
    To my son. What a happy conclusion."

"We must move on the double! My sweetheart's in trouble,"
    Yelled Nebulous, prodding his dad.
"Cause that dirty old man from Milan has a plan,
    And what little I know is all bad."

But as Virtuous rose from his state of repose
    And his lovelies fled into the night,
He sighed, "Phallus, like Pan, never needed a plan
    To deflower a maid in mid-flight.

"I'm not saying its right to chase women for spite
    As the Celt will apparently do,
But it's not a new sport unbeknown to his sort,
    Even though it seems unknown to you.

LeRoy Carl Blake

"And, you might as well learn that it takes more to earn
      The true love of a girl than a rhyme;
While you're hidden away writing poems all day,
      Guys like Phallus are beating your time.

"Now, Vexatious has said he will see us both *dead*
      If you don't give fair Ampla the brush;
What you really must do is think more about *you*
      And how Flatula gave you the rush."

The weight Nebulous bore was now worse than before;
      How could Dad be so wrong about this?
But a glance through the gate helped him shoulder the weight:
      Fleeing Ampla had blown him a kiss.

CHAPTER FIVE

The old Forum rang loud with the din of the crowd
    And the bedlam of daily affairs,
When our lads once again waded through it, and then
    Wound their way to the Palatine Stairs.

"So what happened last night?" urged Pragmaticus, quite
    Shaken up and devoid of all mirth.
"When that creature and you disappeared from our view
    We all thought you were gone from this Earth.

"After all, it was me who was first nominee,
    But I ducked darling Flatula's caper
When you took, in my place, Phallus' pie in the face
    And were then swallowed up in the vapor."

"Thank your gods that you missed that malodorous tryst,"
    Stammered Nebulous, still feeling weak;
"It was *Old, Rotten Cheese with a Bowel Disease*
    In a flatus of garlic and leek."

LeRoy Carl Blake

"But she wanted to *wed*," His best buddy then said,
    "And I feared she had forced you to do it;
But, because she did not, it's a good bet she's hot
    To get back on my case and pursue it."

"You are probably right, but the source of *my* fright,"
    Argued Nebulous, feeling betrayed,
"Is that Phallus, the Celt, plans a notch in his belt
    For your sister and no one's dismayed!"

"Uh, look, Nebulous, first I must tell you the worst:
    Late last night, before going to bed,
My dad called us to meet where we gather to eat
    To announce that fair Ampla shall wed.

"You see, Flatula's scare caught my dad unaware,
    So he sought out a fellow Patrician
With a qualified heir to wed Ampla-the-fair,
    Thus protecting his rank and position.

"And the blue-blood he chose is all right, I suppose
    (But that's merely my own diagnosis);
He's a soldier by trade – though retired from parade –
    Namely General G. Gorgeosus.

NEBULOUS IN LOVE

"Gorgeosus, of course, is a towering force
      In the Senate who hews to Dad's line,
And his soldiering son is now Choice Number One
      For the hand of that sister of mine.

"So, tonight Dad invited the brash – but benighted –
      Young Hunkus Gorgeosus to sup,
When we'll all meet and mingle with Hunk, who's still single,
      In hopes that he'll give it all up."

Oh, how Nebulous shined! "But that means 'til they've dined
      That I still have a chance left to win her!
Oh, I'm saved 'til tonight, because no one will plight
      His or her loving troth before dinner!"

"Ye gods, Nebulous, *quit*! You just torture your wit
      With this hopelessly hopeless bold scheming.
To insist that you stand the least chance for her hand
      Is the fanciest fanciful dreaming.

"You are naught but a poet with no rhymes to show it:
      In terms of known works you're a zero.
But young Hunkus Gorgeosus, almost by osmosis,
      Is Rome's quintessential young hero.

LeRoy Carl Blake

"He is handsome, and wealthy, unspeakably healthy,
      And fought with a conquering Legion;
If you try to compete with the army's elite
      You've your head up your nethermost region!"

This caught Nebulous short as the treasured support
      Of his oldest and truest-blue friend,
Whom he thought would stand fast as he had in the past,
      Met an unceremonious end.

"Well, if that's how you feel, I'll not try to conceal
      That I'm sorry it ended this way.
But I say without doubt, you'll see true love win out;
      She'll be mine at the end of the day."

"Not again!" cried his friend, who was at his wits' end.
      "You'll succeed yet in driving me mad!
When will you understand charming Ampla's fair hand
      Never, ever, was yours to be had?

"To persist in this myth of a love affair with
      My twin sister is dumber than dumb,
When the truth of it is that tonight she'll be *his*,
      And it's never been otherwise, Chum.

NEBULOUS IN LOVE

"I have tried to be kind, knowing lovers are blind,
    And I've helped keep your love poems flowing;
But too much is enough of that juvenile stuff!
    It is time to grow up and get going!"

They arrived at the gate of Vexatious' estate,
    Where poor Nebulous's troubles had started,
And with no obligation for further oration
    Pragmaticus turned and departed.

Feeling spurned and bereft of what hope he'd had left,
    And deserted by even his friend,
Sadly, Nebulous' feet beat a long, slow retreat
    Up the street to his house at the end.

And the rest of his day was spent shuttered away
    As he swore at the gods in frustration,
"Oh, I curse the dark hour when we marry for power
    And true love gets a bum reputation!"

He was still in the throes of his bellicose woes
    When his father arrived, to be greeted
By a mumbled locution of dark retribution
    With expletives all undeleted.

LeRoy Carl Blake

"Would you mind amplifying?" Asked Virtuous, sighing.
    "I don't think I quite got the gist:
Is it Mars that you'll mangle, or Venus you'll strangle,
    Or some other god that I missed?"

"Father, Ampla's been *sold* to a soldier, I'm told,
    By Vexatious, the noble Patrician;
As in piece goods, or cattle, she's merely a chattel
    To barter for higher position."

"Sold?" Virtuous purred. "More like 'promised,' I heard.
    It's the gossip in all the cafés,
And old Georgeus Gorgeosus has made this prognosis:
    She'll marry his son in three days."

But his father's cruel blow hit young Nebulous low –
    Like a ten-libra bag of cement –
In his lonely despair he continued to stare
    In frustration and moan his lament:

"Why do Romans condone – even polish and hone –
    Laws of license where fathers have sway
To give girls in return for the backing they'll earn
    While we poets who love them must stay

NEBULOUS IN LOVE

"Like the dogs in the street, vainly dodging the feet
    Of the rabble who readily give
A quick kick to a cur as if that would deter
    Its determined intention to live."

Again, Virtuous sighed as he gamely replied,
    With uncertainty where he should start,
"Maybe some fathers who seem so brutal to you
    Have their daughters' best interests at heart;

"You say yours is true love, but, by Heaven above!
    If you *had* the girl, what would you do?
Would you feel any better if Grievous had let her
    Wed poor, starving, little old you?

"Son, the gods above know I've no wealth to bestow;
    It's no secret our cupboard is bare.
Now, if you were the sire of this girl you admire,
    Would you put her life into your care?"

The boy sat very still, never moving until
    He looked up and he suddenly said,
"Sir, if I were her sire all her beaux would eat fire,
    Just to prove they were bloody well fed!"

LeRoy Carl Blake

Feeling properly chastened, young Nebulous hastened
    To say he at last saw the light:
"My romantic perception was pure self-deception,
    And you and my best friend were right.

"I was wholly beguiled, and behaved like a child –
    That's the folly that love blindness brings –
From now on it's my plan to behave like a man,
    And I'm putting away childish things.

"And I promise you'll see a huge difference in me
    As I face each new challenging season,
And my poems, I swear, will reflect the new air
    Of my search for true wisdom and reason."

With a heart filled with joy at these words from his boy,
    Aging Virtuous cried, "Oh, my son!
With this promise from you all my dreams have come true.
    Now our future at last has begun!"

And as Virtuous waited while Junior orated,
    He thought to himself, *Ah, touché!*
Such a bright, silver tongue in a mouth still so young
    Surely augurs true greatness some day.

NEBULOUS IN LOVE

"You have made me so proud!" the old solon allowed.
    "Now at last I am free to take aim
Among Rome's nouveau riche for a girl on a leash
    With a father in search of a name.

"Such as mine is – Patrician – to bump his position –
    As he, being flush, will raise mine;
And all you have to do for our dreams to come true
    Is to make her your true valentine."

But the lad spread a grin and said, laughing within,
    "This must be what they call deja vu;
For I thought you just said you expect me to wed
    Just to profit some rich man and you."

"My son," Virtuous said, "You just swore on your head
    To start putting all things in perspective.
Well, a maiden's out there in this city somewhere
    Who needs someone both kind and protective;

"Would you have her succumb to the greed of some bum
    Who would marry her just for her gold,
And then grab what she's got and leave *her* there to rot
    For the rest of her days in the cold?

LeROY CARL BLAKE

"Could you let her pass by knowing you were the guy
        With the chance of a lifetime to save her,
But by being so pure you were forced to demur
        Because cash might have come with the favor?

"Are you saying that I, just because I would try
        To secure for this waif a good pairing,
Should be subject to scorn and, yes, even be shorn
        Of the pittance vouchsafed for my caring?

"Are your morals so steady. . .?" "*So Uncle already!*"
        Cried Nebulous, springing to life.
"Ye gods, Pop, I got it, don't cross it and dot it!
        You're saying you've found me a wife!

"Well, I made you a pact that I'd clean up my act,
        And my word and my bond are the same.
So, to back up my vow I will marry right now –
        By the way, if I may, what's her name?"

"Son, I've kept this on 'hold,' all the while growing old,
        While for years you wrote pretty bon mots;
I cannot name the girl till give it a whirl,
        But you'll be the first Roman to know!

NEBULOUS IN LOVE

"Think on this as we sup," he said, hoisting his cup
        To wash down some coarse bread and boiled suet,
"Very soon we shall dine on the best meats and wine,
        And recline on silk couches to do it."

And while Virtuous told of good things to unfold
        On the day that young Nebulous wed,
Two man-servants of Phallus, dispatched from his palace,
        Arrived with a message, which read:

"Our great lord, the Praefectus, does hereby direct us:
        'Invite (fill in blank) of this 'ouse
To an orgy to honor a 'andsome young goner,
        By reason of takin' a spouse:

"Said carouse to commence at this hour two days 'ence
        At his tony new digs, *Chez Monyeux,*
When Vexatious (the power) and Georgeus (the dower)
        Each gives to the other 'is due.'

"And fair Ampla will swear, 'Eaping fame on her père,
        That her 'eart is pledged cum amorosa
(Which is not all that dumb, seein' 'ow she'll become
        The new Ampla-the-Fair Gorgeosa.")

LeRoy Carl Blake

The lad spun toward his dad and he screamed, "Are they *mad?*
    They are sending my blossoming flower
To the Celt's cunning care in his palace, and there
    To be plucked like a rose from his bower!

"Can't you fools understand? That debaucher has planned
    This whole plot as a ruse to beguile her!
Is Vexatious so blind to the Celt's wanton mind
    He can't see through this scheme to defile her?

"Why, that dirty old Gaul has outsmarted you all,
    And Pragmaticus too, I regret,
For indeed it was he who this day assured *me*
    That the Celt was no longer a threat.

"*We must stop him!*" he cried, leaping up to collide
    With a standard which bore a confection
Of thick cream and fresh fruits, mixed with berries and shoots,
    Which went flying in every direction.

In a flash the boy split like a bat from the Pit
    As the goo flew all over the place,
While the messengers stared, neither having been spared,
    And poor Virtuous buried his face.

NEBULOUS IN LOVE

"As you may 'ave observed, your dessert 'as been served,"
    Said the messenger doing the talking,
"And, that bein' the case, by your ven'rable grace,
    We'll be setting our sandals to walking."

And removing wild berries, sliced peaches and cherries
    From sticky, wet tunics, they tore
Like fruit salad in flight on a creamy delight
    Through the senator's house to his door.

Only Virtuous stayed, sinking deeper in shade
    With a heart that was heavy as lead,
As he watched all his dreams split apart at the seams
    Yet again *and again!* in his head.

Now completely undone by his frivolous son
    In whom hope had so recently risen,
The man heard himself say, "I am *damned* if I'll stay
    One more day in his rhyme-riddled prison!"

CHAPTER SIX

In the long, narrow street of the Roman elite
    Where the dwellings were few but first rate,
A fresh torch, burning bright, laid a path through the night
    To a very imposing front gate.

Hiding there in the dark, just beyond the lamp's arc,
    Our young Nebulous, true to his being,
Was inspecting that door, unresolved to the core
    About opting for staying or fleeing.

Fear for Ampla dear's fate had delivered him straight
    To Pragmaticus' gate in the night,
But if Grievous found out he was nosing about
    He'd be *carnis mortuus* on sight.

But while Nebulous waited with fear unabated,
    Up swaggered a handsome young jock;
He was built like a god and stood straight as a rod
    As he stopped at the portal to knock.

NEBULOUS IN LOVE

When the gate opened wide our young Nebulous *died*
    From the blow to his teenager's psyche,
For the stud standing there with the soldierly air
    Must be Hunkus, all edgy and spiky.

Oh, how Nebulous hurt! His poor heart bit the dirt
    At the hopelessness, now, of his mission;
For Vexatious, of course, had endorsed the right horse:
    Hunk was clearly beyond competition.

Dammit! Hunkus can wait! I've too much on my plate
    To make room for that soldier at all;
And the reason I've come doesn't bear on that bum,
    But on stopping the fat man from Gaul!

He crept up to the door he had watched heretofore,
    Which he found had been left off the latch,
And he crossed, with a smile, the cold stone peristyle
    To the atrium hall with dispatch.

Then he slipped through that room to the triclinium,
    Where he opened the door just a crack;
To his utter surprise he stared into ten eyes,
    The five owners of which stared right back.

LeRoy Carl Blake

The great Grievous lay prone on a couch all alone,
    And his guest was alone on another,
While fair Ampla sat, gracing a low table, facing
    The smiles of her mother and brother.

The girl's eyes were aglaze as she focused her gaze
    On the stud of her dear daddy's choosing,
And acknowledged no more of the boy at the door
    Than a blur interrupting her musing.

But Vexatious saw red when the strange, curly head
    Popped in view in his sanctum sanctorum,
And he screamed at his guard, "Have him skewered and tarred!"
    For the ultimate breach of decorum.

Ah, but *Hunkus* was quicker than any guard's sticker
    (although they were aimed for their throws).
When he leaped to the door, scarcely touching the floor,
    And hauled Nebulous in by his nose.

"And just what have we here?" Hunkus asked with a sneer,
    Lifting Nebulous high by his snout;
"It does seem a bit late to be crashing the gate;
    Tell us, why are you mucking about?"

NEBULOUS IN LOVE

"By the gods, it's that brat!" bellowed Grievous, whereat
    The great Hunkus paraded his booty,
And poor Nebulous, squealing, was held to the ceiling,
    Relieving his feet of their duty.

"Please let go of by doze," he cried out in the throes
    Of distress as he twisted in pain,
With his mangled proboscis held high by Colossus,
    His pride very much down the drain.

"Why, you damnable punk!" spat the Senator. "Hunk,
    His intrusion here more than just rankles:
He was warned once before not to darken this door
    Or I'd part his hair down to his ankles."

"But, you dode understa'd! I've dud duthigh that's bad,
    I just wadded to talk to Pragbaddicus!
Wohd you *please* put be dowd with by feet odd the growd,
    'Cause by corpus is dot aerostaddicus!"

"You young insolent bum, it's for Ampla you've come,
    So don't start with that tedious ploy!
I'm not quite so naïve as to ever believe
    That you came here to talk to my boy!"

LeRoy Carl Blake

Then to Hunkus he said, "By the hair on my head
    His intentions are clearer than clear:
He believes he's your rival, although his survival
    Was doomed when he showed up in here."

"What!" The soldier was shocked that this bumpkin held locked
    By the nose in his fist would presume
To inhale the same air never mind that he'd dare
    To compete to be fair Ampla's groom.

"You mean this petty ass puts himself in *my* class?
    I don't sing my own praises, but then,
In one glorious year I've done more with one spear
    Than this fool could accomplish with ten!

"I have tramped with our legions to unholy regions,
    And fought to the death with our foes,
And I've climbed through the ranks with the kudos and thanks
    Of the greatest commanders Rome knows.

"At the Delta Defile they commended my style
    As I rose like a man to the call,
And alone penetrated the stronghold once rated
    The tightest maneuver of all!

NEBULOUS IN LOVE

"And if *I* hadn't been in the van going in
      When we stormed the impregnable breastwork,
Who indeed would have measured the frontage we treasured,
      And then volunteered for the test work?

"And, yes, wasn't it *I who*, last Fourth of July,
      On the shores of the Sellibah Sea,
With a firm, hard command, took the matter in hand
      And defeated the dreaded Ennui?"

"Oh ye gods, Thad's edough!" Was then heard in a huff.
      "If you wahd to impress us, you widd!
But you soud like by father, who's really a bother –
      Dow, dabbit, let go of by skidd!"

Hunkus stopped by the chair of sweet Ampla, and there
      Propelled Nebulous into her view;
Then, while keeping him stranded he sneered and demanded,
      "You really thought she'd prefer *you?*"

Then he opened his fist as he blithely dismissed
      The proboscis with careless dispatchment;
So the nose hit the dirt, but what caused the real hurt
      Was the crash of its larger attachment.

LeRoy Carl Blake

"Take that garbage away! That's enough for one day,"
    Ordered Grievous while pouring more wine.
After draining his cup he continued to sup,
    Bidding Hunkus again to recline.

But as Hunkus lay down he felt sure he would drown
    In the gaze of his young ingénue
And said, "Nebulous, there, is a bit of a square."
    And fair Ampla said, "Nebulous who?"

Meanwhile, Nebulous' nose could have posed for a hose,
    Or at least for an umbrella holder;
As he shakily rose recomposing his clothes,
    A gendarme put the arm on his shoulder.

But, at seeing his buddy about to get bloody,
    Pragmaticus, daring to speak,
Blurted, "Pater, in sooth he is telling the truth:
    It is I whom he came here to seek."

The young son-and-heir stood as he properly should,
    And he spoke to a withering glare:
"I regret his intrusion on sovereign seclusion;
    I simply forgot he was there.

NEBULOUS IN LOVE

"But if you will agree that my friend may go free
      To return to his own habitation,
I will send him away where I promise he'll stay
      After we've had a brief conversation."

So then, Grievous, distracted by thoughts more protracted
      Of power about to accrue,
Merely nodded his head and Pragmaticus fled,
      Whisking Nebulous quickly from view.

The boys scrambled outside where Pragmaticus sighed
      To the friend whom he found so dismaying:
"Now that I've saved your butt will you please tell me what
      Is the name of the game you are playing?"

"Oh, my friend, it's no game! On my dear mother's name,
      Our position's extremely extreme,
For your sister, you felt, would be safe from the Celt,
      But tonight I have learned of his scheme."

"By a 'scheme' do you mean that a theme unforeseen
      Is the reason for Phallus' reception?
Well now, Phallus is quick, but his orgy's no trick
      Or my dad would have seen the deception.

LeRoy Carl Blake

"Phallus couldn't succeed in a seedy misdeed,
    Notwithstanding his dark predilection,
For my sister, you'll see, will be safe as can be
    With her Hunkus around for protection."

"No! No!" Nebulous said, sternly shaking his head.
    "You are still underrating the Gaul!
If he's outguessed your father, it won't be a bother
    To get around Hunkus at all!"

"So? What's your concern? Are you still on a burn
    To win Ampla by dint of volition?
If you are, you're too late, and you still wouldn't rate
    Without money and land and position."

But young Nebulous knew the respect he was due
    And politely enlightened his friend:
"Prag, I do understand about money and land:
    You've explained it and I comprehend;

"But the Ludicrous name, which lays claim to great fame,
    Provides all the 'position' required;
What I also can see is that *she* must stay free
    While the land and the cash are acquired!"

NEBULOUS IN LOVE

In the early hour's damp by the flickering lamp,
    Grim Pragmaticus turned from the light
To conceal his cold fears from this friend of ten years
    Who was losing his world on this night.

"Pal, I'm sorry to say, be your name what it may,
    You've been totally put out of action;
Though he may be outwitted, my dad is committed,
    And honor precludes a retraction.

"Even that's not the worst – you should hear it here first –
    Yes, my sister's in love with the Hunk.
And she can't take her eyes off his pecs and his thighs,
    Though I think he's a self-centered punk.

"And the pitiful state of my own sorry fate
    Is that Flatula's hot on my tail:
Pater's tried every contact to back-date a contract,
    But not yet to any avail.

"So, I'm sorry, my friend, but I've nothing to lend
    In the way of encouraging cheer;
Now I'd better return to ease Pater's concern,
    Or risk having him find you're still here."

LeRoy Carl Blake

Then, without saying more, he ducked back through the door
      To the haughty Vexatious abode,
Where he waved a goodnight and then closed the door tight
      And was gone from the cold, lonely road.

Back again in the night with his unresolved plight,
      Slowly Nebulous started to go,
And felt very much older – was everything colder? –
      Than just a few minutes ago.

The same torch as before threw his shadow once more
      Down the long, narrow cobblestone street,
But his heart was a rock in the numb aftershock
      Of his ironbound, solid defeat.

But the most painful aching was due to his waking
      To learn, as his friend knew he must,
That he'd squandered his prime writing frivolous rhyme
      While his future lay ground in the dust.

CHAPTER SEVEN

The dawn flooded his room, but young Nebulous' gloom
    Didn't yield to the brightness at all,
For last night's hasty pledge left him out on a ledge
    From which now he was certain he'd fall.

He half staggered from bed with an ache in his head
    And a prayer to the gods to prolong
Their nocturnal protection from his predilection
    To always, it seems, get it wrong.

And on reaching the room called the triclinium
    For his morning repast in repose,
He was filled with chagrin when his father walked in
    And said, "What the hell's wrong with your nose?"

Now he really felt rotten. He'd nearly forgotten
    His schnoz which was throbbing away,
So, avoiding the thread of the subject, he said,
    "Nothing much. So, what's on for today?"

LeROY CARL BLAKE

Replied Virtuous, staring at that which was glaring
    In tones of bright red, blue, and gray,
"Where've you been, on the Moon? Or inside a cocoon?
    This is Dubius' Triumphal day.

"All of Rome will be there at the stadium stair,
    Or the Circus, or Triumphal Gate,
And if we're to arrive in one piece and alive,
    We'll be better off early than late."

Of course Nebulous knew what that meant he must do:
    He must escort his father, "The Senator;"
How on earth could he see his fair sweetheart if he
    Had to sit with his stodgy progenitor?

But he quickly recovered ere Pater discovered
    His Dubius feelings, which were:
That as generals go he was less than so-so,
    And Despoticus, too, must concur.

If not, why would he make honored Dubius take
    All his bows in a one-day parade,
When great triumphs of old took three days to unfold
    Before all of the loot was displayed?

NEBULOUS IN LOVE

But he said to his dad, "I am truthfully glad
    For the laurels the great man is due:
Leaving no stone unturned he has raped, robbed and burned
    Till I'm *flushed* with emotion. Aren't you?

"And with thousands of horses supporting his forces,
    And thousands and thousands of heroes,
I can get such a thrill that it gives me a chill
    Just in adding up all of those zeroes.

"And the blare of the trumpets, the strut of the strumpets,
    The pomp that attends the affair,
And the miles of manure all those horses are sure
    To contribute to season the air

"Make me swell up with pride and get all teary-eyed
    To be part of the great Roman state,
And it then makes me laugh at that fool-and-a-half
    In whose honor we'll all celebrate."

But his father was not buying into the plot
    Of avoiding the issue this day;
He said, "Shut up and eat and then get on your feet.
    You've last night to explain on the way."

So now Nebulous, mad that his resolute dad
      Wouldn't let him get out of his sight,
And beset by the stress from the bitch of a mess
      He had got himself into last night,

Left his house in a pet and with Virtuous set
      A straight course down a different stair
(Not the one that goes down to the Forum, in town,
      But a narrow, less formal affair

With just two minor bends that descends till it ends
      At the old Circus Maximus, where
The great show would unfold as in Triumphs of old,
      With some leaves stuck in somebody's hair).

And, as father and son, yielding yardage to none,
      Fought the flood of the Circus-bound throng,
Every passing face rose to scan Nebulous' nose,
      And then laugh before moving along.

"If they start giving prizes for nasal disguises,"
      Said Virtuous, "you'll win the day.
Now, by Jupiter's light, just where *were* you last night,
      And just how did your beak get that way?"

NEBULOUS IN LOVE

"Father, I can well see that you're angry with me
        For behavior that seems dualistic,
But if Ampla-the-dear isn't warned to keep clear,
        She will wind up a Celtic statistic.

"Nothing new has transpired, things are still just as mired
        In the muck that Vexatious created;
My girl's still going to marry that dumb functionary
        Whose parents should never have mated.

"And, ere that fateful day, I'm heartbroken to say,
        The Old Celt will have done as he's able.
All the cards have been played; all that's left, I'm afraid,
        Is to pick up the chips from the table."

As the mob swept the pair down the elegant stair,
        The old senator fumed, "You won't tell me?
All I wanted to know was where you deigned to go
        After dinner, but now you compel me

"To do that which I could have, and certainly should have,
        Long since to get out of this rut:
I am hitching you, Kiddo, to Rome's richest widow –
        That is, if she'll bid on your butt.

LeRoy Carl Blake

"I am fed up with living my days to keep giving
    Your romance control of my life;
From now on you will pay every inch of the way
    From the dowry I'll get from your wife.

"So be warned, my young blade: Ere this stupid parade
    Confirms Rome's newest laureate winner,
I'll cash in on your oath and arrange your damned troth
    Per your promise last night before dinner!"

The words struck like a dart at young Nebulous' heart!
    He had never heard Pater so strident.
Was it true? Was he through? What the hell could he *do*
    To jump out of the way of this trident?

With his poet's dumb luck he had managed to duck
    All the slings and the arrows before,
And he'd come to believe in each fateful reprieve,
    But he sure wasn't sure any more.

Oh, ye gods! the lad thought as he mentally fought
    For a way to get out of his deadlock,
For what good would it be if sweet Ampla went free,
    If then *he* should be sold into wedlock?

NEBULOUS IN LOVE

At the Circus they fled to an entry which led
      'Neath the seats of the Roman elite,
And escaped from the crush to a cold, stony hush
      And the sandal-soled slap of their feet

To emerge at the tiers where the Senator's peers
      Were arranging themselves by their faction,
Which meant Virtuous' Claque sat way up in the back,
      While Vexatious was down near the action.

Then the crowd stood and roared for the man they adored:
      He who heard all the noise without heeding
Through a stupefied grin and the drool on his chin
      As he drank through the entire proceeding.

And while Nebulous craned with the others who strained
      For a peek in the Emperor's stall,
He caught sight of his friend, down in front, on the end,
      But his friend wasn't watching at all.

For Pragmaticus' eyes held a worthier prize,
      Which had set his young heartstrings afire;
And she, too, sat below in the very front row,
      Next to Georgeus Gorgeosus, her sire.

LeRoy Carl Blake

It was clearer than clear, even high in the rear
      (Not one horny old solon had missed her)
That Pragmaticus had, right in front of her dad,
      Been bedazzled by Hunkus' kid sister.

With no hope for tomorrow and real, profound sorrow,
      Young Nebulous watched in despair;
For Pragmaticus' love, like his own turtledove,
      Would, alas, disappear in thin air.

Just as greedy, audacious, self-serving Vexatious
      Bestowed Ampla's fair hand on another,
So the wine merchant laid his own foul-feathered maid
      On Pragmaticus, Ampla's twin brother.

But his foremost concern was his own rotten turn
      On the wheel of misfortune that day,
And he thought he would drown, as the people calmed down,
      In the depths of his deepest dismay.

In this new state of mind he was startled to find
      The first token of Virtuous' guile;
For his dad's ugly frown had been turned upside down,
      And replaced by a smug little smile.

NEBULOUS IN LOVE

Feigning idle distraction to hide his reaction
        To where his old man turned his focus,
He tracked Virtuous' eye – like a recondite spy –
        To a stall in the proximus locus.

There, two women of means, like rare, fine figurines,
        With their backs to our clandestine pair,
Were reclined near the wall neath a huge parasol
        While a servant stood fanning the air.

From where Nebulous sat it was obvious that
        The poseur on the left was a hooter:
She was baring more skin, she was stylishly thin,
        And in all, she was probably cuter;

Also, she on the left wasn't wholly bereft
        By the gods, who had left her endowed
With big, come-hither eyes which she laid on the guys
        Like a streetwalker working the crowd.

So, our Nebulous knew it could only be true
        (By the drop-dead couture that she wore,
Plus her manicured nails and some other details
        That bespoke flowing coffers galore)

LeROY CARL BLAKE

That the one on the *right* would be his by tonight
        If his father could pull off the deal,
And he asked himself, *how is she husbandless now*
        If her assets are really for real?

Facing certain disaster, he drove his brain faster
        And stared at the back of her head,
While he struggled to think, as he sped toward the brink,
        Of the words that Pragmaticus said:

"So, enough is enough," he had yelled in a huff,
        "It is time to get on with your life!"
But now *what could he do* in the minute or two
        Ere the gods made this woman his wife?

The first marchers appeared while the mob stood and cheered
        For each helmeted brave Roman rover,
And the woman whose rear had so dampened his cheer
        Turned to watch – and he damned near fell over.

Our boy's senses took flight at the jaw-dropping sight,
        For her profile, however presented,
Radiated a shock that would cock-up a clock
        (Well, it would had the clock been invented).

NEBULOUS IN LOVE

The first soldiers passed by with their banners held high
      And their armor ablaze in the sun,
But all Nebulous saw was a great, gaping maw
      Poised to swallow his life, unbegun.

But the marchers kept coming: *A hundred guys drumming!*
      Folks cheered 'til their faces turned blue
(They could all have been lawyers or plumbers and sawyers
      For all the great hoi polloi knew),

Then the rank-and-file ranks who had angst for the thanks
      And the praises they knew they deserved,
Were all followed at length by the aggregate strength
      Of the staff of the gen'ral they served.

For our Nebulous, though, the parade down below
      Might as well have been held in the dark;
Just one look at *that face* was enough to erase
      The last ember of hope's tiny spark.

The crowd came to their feet as the mounted elite
      Packed the Circus with corps upon corps,
And the musclebound power of Rome's finest flower
      Kept everyone screaming for more.

Then at last, the Big Plum! The grand moment had come,
      For now Dubius rode into view:
The crowd hiked up the din as their hero breezed in
      With an escort of fifty-and-two

Of the handsomest creatures with bronzed, Roman features,
      Their armor all shiny and clean,
That the crowds in their seats or the mobs in the streets
      Ever hoped to have heard of or seen.

Then, *the sight of one man* in the general's van
      Broke the spell of the mighty hypnosis:
For there, sitting astraddle his rich, Roman saddle
      Was Hunkus – *ye gods!* – Gorgeosus.

Just the soldierly essence of Hunkus's presence
      Was fit to make Nebulous fry,
And Pragmaticus' charge to "grow up" was writ large
      In his mind as the warrior rode by.

And he swore by his wits he'd climb out of the pits
      Where his prodigal folly had led,
And wind up, as they say, at the end of the day
      With the Girl of his Dreams in his bed.

NEBULOUS IN LOVE

Then, like Phoenix a-borning that clear, lucid morning,
    He saw what he needed to do:
One: Become very rich, to the measure of which
    He would *bury* the soldier, and Two:

Find a scheme to expel that damn he-man-from-Hell
    From the dreams of sweet Ampla right now!
(Coming up with the "What" made him feel better, but
    He'd feel much better still with the "How.")

As the horses departed the Circus and started
    The long, post-Triumphal retreat,
He heard Virtuous say in his own quiet way,
    "There is someone I want you to meet."

But his moment of truth had undraped callow youth
    Like a shroud from the now-mature man,
And he suddenly knew what exactly to do
    In the ever-diminishing span

Of the seconds until he'd be auctioned at will
    To that fright'ning old woman to wed,
And torpedo his life with a hatchet-faced wife
    When he wanted fair Ampla instead.

So, he swallowed his dread and to Virtuous said,
        "Pater mine, I can do this alone.
Just supply me her name: *I'll* propose to the dame
        (And enlist a new twist of my own!).

"If you'll please step aside and not trample my pride,
        I believe you will find there's no need
For your old fashioned way: All I need is to say
        'I am Ludicrous' and she'll accede."

"If her name you don't know," whispered Virtuous, low,
        So the lady could not overhear,
"You are out of your mind, for to even the blind
        Hideosa's foul face should be clear.

"So don't give me some lip about how you're so hip
        That you'll handle this thing with aplomb;
If you blow it, my boy, I will rend you with joy
        Just as soon as I get your butt home!"

Thus, young Nebulous said to his sire, "Go ahead.
        You may trust me or not as you will,
I must fly to the side of my storybook bride
        Ere *she* flies up the Palatine Hill."

NEBULOUS IN LOVE

Then he turned with an air of contempt for his père
      As he gathered his toga in style,
And he strode to the place where he'd witnessed *that face*
      While compelling his own face to smile.

"Lovely ladies," he said, never turning his head
      From a view that would test mother-love,
"May I have your consent to most humbly present
      My most Ludicrous family, whereof,

"Since the first days of Rome – before kings called it home –
      It was proven that our blood was blue,
Which indeed it remains, coursing pure in our veins,
      Pulsing honest, brave-hearted and true."

"Well I'm sure that it does! You must get such a *buzz*,"
      Cooed the one on the left in repose.
Hideosa, however, made no such endeavor;
      She said, "What the hell's with your nose?

"You look like a baboon from the South Cameroon
      Who got beat in a fight," she said smugly.
"Your damn blood may be blue, but it can't touch the hue
      Of your beak, which is red-white-and-ugly."

LeRoy Carl Blake

He was taken aback at Miss Pulchritude's lack
    Of a grasp of what he was pursuing;
He said meekly, "That's right, I got hurt in a fight –
    Now, may I please get on with my wooing?"

With a thrust of her hips and her tongue through her lips,
    The much younger one said, "Don't mind *her*.
I just think it's divine that a handsome young swine
    With blue blood wants to call on us, sir."

"It is '*swain*,' you born twit!" Spectra spat in a fit,
    "And he's not here to call upon *us*!
When the blue-blooded needy get hungry and greedy
    They fester like rivers of pus;

"They come out of the walls and they fill up the halls
    Of the fisc'ly fit widows like me,
And they think we're so stupid we think it was Cupid
    Who sent them around to have tea.

"Well, you're far, far too young – I don't care how you're hung" –
    She said, looking our lad in the eye;
"Though I've said I would maim for a blue-blooded name,
    I must cordially bid *you* good-bye."

NEBULOUS IN LOVE

"I don't think he's too young," said the one with the tongue
      And the marvelous, come-hither eye.
"If he gets you unstrung then *I'll* see how he's hung."
      And, so saying, her hand found his thigh.

And her smug little smile when he jumped half a mile
      Proved her probe wasn't wholly in vain,
And she sighed, "Yeah, you're right, he's still young and uptight,
      But he'd be kinda kinky to train."

"Cut that out!" our boy cried through the shreds of his pride
      And the swagger with which he had started,
"I'm not talking to you so just shut up and shoo!
      I'll not finish until you've departed!"

But he trembled with rage at their scorn for his age
      And the gall of that easy-eyed frail;
And he vowed he would stand his own ground and demand
      That his offer be heard in detail.

Hideosa then waved for the cute – but depraved –
      Younger woman to lessen the ruction:
"Take the servants and split; I'll just sit here a bit,
      While I hear his big plan for seduction.

LeRoy Carl Blake

"Now, let's have it, young man – be as brief as you can –
    What in me do you find so worthwhile?
I'm as ugly as wrath and, ere Saturday's bath,
    I smell worse than I look by a mile;

"And my blood isn't blue; I'm much older than you;
    And in public I scratch where I itch;
So please tell me, I pray, for I really can't stay,
    Could it possibly be that I'm... rich?"

"Ah, Fair Lady," he said, through a face turning red,
    "You have seen my proposal straight through,
For your great intellect, which I'll ne'er disaffect,
    Is the gift I most cherish in you.

"For now haven't you just, with a sharp, mental thrust,
    Penetrated the heart of the beast,
Which confirms I am right: You have loads of insight
    (And of gold, which I want mentioned least)."

"So, you're after my brain," Spectra sneered with disdain,
    Keeping Nebulous firmly at bay.
"If you're into that blather, I'm sure I would rather
    Stop talking and be on my way.

NEBULOUS IN LOVE

"But if we can be clear that the reason you're here
      Is the cash overflowing my coffer,
We can cut to the scene where you fin'lly come clean
      And reveal what's contained in your offer."

Feeling thoroughly cowed, somber Nebulous bowed
      To her pure, perspicacious perception:
"Gracious lady," said he, "Pray have patience with me,
      For I've tried from the very inception

"Of our meeting today not to lead you astray,
      But to stay with accepted convention;
But we've journeyed apart – with the help of that tart –
      From my natural, noble intention.

"So, suffice it to say on this Triumphal day,
      That the gist of my offer is this:
Your great whacking estate in exchange for a mate
      Who will give you great love and true bliss;

"A fine man who will bring, with a gold wedding ring,
      So much joy from the gods up above,
You will find very soon ev'ry pathway bestrewn
      With the roses of heavenly love;

LeRoy Carl Blake

"A great man, in his prime, who has known in his time
      All the powers-that-be in the Senate,
And, if not for his rank lack of funds in the bank,
      Would have authored his own Roman Tenet;

"And now, last but not least, he's a limitless feast
      Of the virtues and values of Rome,
Who would rather be dead than to have on his head
      Any hint of a scandal at home."

Spectra stirred where she lay and said softly, "Touché.
      Such a man would be one among few.
To be such a man's wife would give meaning to life;
      But so what? All I see here is you."

The boy hid his chagrin at her belt to the chin,
      For the pay-off for all of his bother
Was about to be named: He then grandly proclaimed,
      "I propose in the name of . . . my father."

"Do you mean," Spectra said, "You expect me to wed
      Some old man with his future behind him?
While it's true he's respected, he's also rejected
      By rules of the Senate that bind him

NEBULOUS IN LOVE

"To the hinter-most ranks with the kooks and the cranks
    Where nobody important can find him,
While he wastes his best years in the shade of his peers
    'Neath the tread of the millstones that grind him.

"Or perhaps you infer I should gladly concur
    With your plan to surrender my treasure
For the privilege of the illusion of love
    In the place of a lifetime of pleasure?

"Or it may be, somehow, you believe this old frau,
    Whose façade looks like Lucifer drew it,
Is so bored on the shelf she'd hump Hades himself
    If he'd just take her money to do it?

"Or perhaps 'twas all three, Like a rich potpourri
    Of the scenes I depicted above,
Made you think I'd be willing to give every shilling
    In awe at your worship thereof?

"I'm afraid I can't play at your jackstraws today,
    And you've only your ego to blame:
Had your suit been well planned – not so brashly off-hand –
    You'd have asked what conditions *I* claim."

LeROY CARL BLAKE

As she started to leave the boy clutched at her sleeve;
    Oh my god! Is she walking away?
"What conditions are those? *What have you to disclose?*
    Dearest lady, please say that you'll stay!"

"Ah, my brave little friend, please don't try to pretend
    You don't know that young tart was my sister.
My condition, my lad, to say 'yes' to your dad:
    Find that harlot a permanent mister!

"I am tired of that bitch and her lickerish itch,
    Like a housecat in heat on the make;
For to her, 'daily bred' doesn't mean getting fed –
    I don't know how much more I can take!

"I have harbored that slut and put clothes on her butt
    Since the day that our dear Mother died,
When the Temple devout caught her there, putting out,
    Before tears from the fun'ral had dried.

"She spread wide for a pass at my husband, alas,
    Who had planned to go deep in reception
Till I got in between with a one-woman screen
    And pulled off the great pass interception.

NEBULOUS IN LOVE

"In the days I was wedded I happily bedded
      My man when he wanted me to,
But Coita, the bimbo, with legs spread akimbo,
      Can't stop between *sets* for 'I do.'

"The condition then stands: I want *her* off my hands,
      Safely married and out of the way
Before I will agree to your dad wedding me.
      Now, do I have a 'Yea' or a 'Nay?'"

Trembling, Nebulous stood facing Spectra, who could
      Make or break his whole life on this day,
And he smothered his fears as he sent to her ears
      A faint-hearted – but welcome – "It's Yea."

Spectra's gaze was benign as she purred, "Well, that's fine.
      I'll expect to meet your nominee
Whose finesse will, in fact, change Coita's bad act
      Before Virtuous comes courting me."

She extended her hand, which he kissed as he scanned
      All her jewelry (none of it *faux*)
And he thought, as he bent with his lips to cement
      Their agreement, *one down, one to go.*

LeRoy Carl Blake

He had solved problem A in a masterful way,
    Though he'd left his old man up a tree;
Then he hastened to think, *Wasn't Dad at the brink*
    Of inflicting the same thing on me?

Thus, his thoughts turned with zest to his plan for that pest
    Of a soldier he thoroughly hated,
And how soon he'd be free of that jerk (problem B),
    As he strolled to where Virtuous waited.

"What on Earth did you say? *She is walking away!*"
    Gasped his father, demanding an answer.
"Did she sanction your suit? Or did you get the boot
    With your boyish attempts to romance her?"

"Not to worry, dear sir! Although wont to demur,"
    Offered Nebulous, gaining composure,
"She agreed to the fete, but then afterward set
    A condition to meet before closure:

"She shall not be paid court until I can report
    That I've done what she wants me to do:
Her kid sister, a champ of an all-around tramp,
    Must be given a new husband, too."

NEBULOUS IN LOVE

"Have you gone raving *mad?* Every man in Rome's had
      A carouse with that curb-service doxy!
When one took a day off she proceeded to boff
      A gorilla sent in as his proxy."

"Yes, I know, and I fear that the message is clear:
      There's no cash in it for the duration,
Until we can recruit some galoot of a brute
      Unencumbered by her reputation."

"But Son, where will we look?" Asked the Senator, shook
      At the prospect of failing once more
To deliver the goods and get out of the woods,
      And to beat back the wolf from the door.

"Sire, I'd fain go down there to the foot of this stair,
      Where Pragmaticus stares into space;
He's a very hip guy and I'm sure, if he'll try,
      He can quote the exact time and place

"Where our stud-horse will wait for his foredestined date
      With Coita of fable and myth,
Upon being presented, all bathed, buffed, and scented,
      For Spectra's approval forthwith."

LeROY CARL BLAKE

Whereupon, saying that, he lit out like a bat
    Leaving Virtuous standing alone,
And he loped down the tiers through the Senator's peers
    To his friend, whose new sweetheart had flown.

Poor Pragmaticus' heart had been sundered apart
    By the girl he had watched in repose,
And as Nebulous neared, said Pragmaticus: "Weird!
    What in Hades is wrong with your nose?"

"Has your sense taken flight? Harken back to last night!"
    Blurted Nebulous, painfully hurt.
"This damn polychrome knob was a customized job
    From that jerk with the sheet metal shirt!"

"Ah, forgive me, old chum, but my brain's on the bum,"
    Said his friend in that droll way of his,
"And my head's not the same since I learned that her name
    Is Delicia (Gorgeosa, that is)."

"Yeah, Delicia's de-lish, and she's really your dish.
    Why, she'd be a real dream as your wife.
But with Flatula there in your future somewhere,
    You can dream her right out of your life.

NEBULOUS IN LOVE

"But I didn't just run down this stairway for fun!
      No! I hurried to bring you this scoop:
I've secured all the cash that I'll need in my stash
      To knock Grievous – your dad – for a loop.

"Now the problem at hand isn't money or land,
      But that Hunkus-the-Hero remains;
So what I want to do is to try to help you
      In exchange for the use of *your* brains.

"I make no guarantees; I'll just talk to the Sleaze
      To find out if there's some earthly way
To fit Flatula's fate to some other great mate
      For a blue-blooded nuptial day."

"If you're offering me a real chance to be free
      From that wine merchant's odious whelp,
Then I promise you'll see just how good I can be,"
      Swore Pragmaticus, vowing to help.

"Then it's done! It's begun! We're united as one,"
      Shouted Nebulous, pumping the hand
Of the youth he was sure the gods sent to secure
      The great coup he'd so cunningly planned.

LeRoy Carl Blake

"I'll go straight to the deed! Wish me Mercury's speed!
      I'll find Sleazum's wine stall in the mart,
Where he may change his view and take pity on you
      From the depths of his kind merchant's heart.

"And remember, my friend, that this day must not end
      Without sharing with me what you've done
Toward a plan to achieve getting Hunkus to leave
      Ere tomorrow night's orgy's begun."

Then Pragmaticus said, "I so swear by my head!
      Though we can't meet again on this day,
For my father's whole tribe must all eat and imbibe
      While we toast the night hours away

"With the Hunk and his clan to the very last man,
      Which will last until Bacchus knows when;
So we'll have to hang tight till tomorrow's first light,
      And we'll meet at your father's house then."

When Vexatious had gone his whole clan had withdrawn,
      And Pragmaticus hurried to catch them,
Leaving Nebulous there launching dreams in the air
      With the prospect, at last, that he'd hatch them.

CHAPTER EIGHT

Now, the first light of dawn had long since come and gone,
    And young Nebulous, starting to pace,
Cursed his long, enforced wait as the morning grew late,
    For his friend had not yet shown his face.

But, although it was true his pal hadn't come through –
    What was holding him up, anyway?—
The real reason he burned was because he'd been spurned
    When he met with the Sleaze yesterday:

"You irrelevant square! What the hell do you care
    Whom I choose for my daughter to wed?"
The wine seller had screamed while our lad stood and steamed.
    "Go on back up your Hill and *drop dead*!

"It is not up to you to say who can pursue
    The Vexatious successor and heir;
So just take my advice – I will say it real nice –
    And keep out of what's left of my hair!"

LeRoy Carl Blake

Sneered our Nebulous, "Please! Grievous' proud legatees
    Aren't the only blue bloods of renown!
Worldly wealth and wide fame attend many a name
    Of the arrogant snobs in this town.

"Surely somebody who is as artful as you,
    With the minimum quotient of brains,
Has discerned that the mob with whom you would hobnob
    Is chock full of such suitable swains?

"So, be out with the truth! Any blue-blooded youth
    For your daughter is all that you need,
And you couldn't care less if the guy is a mess
    Just as long as the two interbreed."

Then in hushed, whispered tones from way down in his bones
    The old merchant confided, "That's true –
But Patricians will not socialize with our lot,
    As you know, since your own blood is blue,

"Unless we of the town catch a swell with 'em down
    And persuade him to see things our way,
Which I've managed to do with Vexatious, so you
    Needn't pain yourself further. Good day!"

NEBULOUS IN LOVE

So, the best he had wrung from the merchant's sharp tongue
    Was a balky admission, to wit:
Any rich man would do if his blood were pure blue,
    But no blue blood had deigned to commit.

Thus, his problems, now twain, were both: how to obtain,
    Short of raiding slave markets and galleys,
Willing mates for *two* skirts – one who farts, one who flirts –
    Without cruising for drunks in dark alleys.

But while Nebulous faced all his woes as he paced,
    There arose such a din at the door,
That he opened it wide, quickly stepping aside,
    As Pragmaticus sprawled on the floor.

"Ho, Pragmaticus, come!" Cried our lad to his chum.
    "I've been waiting for over an hour!
I had started to fear that you wouldn't appear.
    Say, why is it you're looking so sour?"

"I don't look half as bad as I feel, my good lad,"
    Said his friend as he got to his feet,
"Though I've not hit the hay since we met yesterday,
    And I'm more than a tiny bit beat.

LeRoy Carl Blake

"But first, let me explain why you waited in vain
    When I didn't show up right away;
Stupid Hunkus orated all night, unabated,
    Till well after night turned to day!

"And while we were constrained to be thus entertained
    Through the hours by that bellicose bore,
I just tuned out the drone with some thoughts of my own
    About how to show Hunkus the door.

"But we've gotta talk fast, 'cause I'm not gonna last,
    And I barely can see through these eyes;
"So let's start with you, friend: How did you, in the end,
    Cut the wine merchant down to our size?"

"Oh, uh, *Sleazum*. Um, yes. Well, I have to confess
    You're not out of the woods yet, of course,
But I did make him state he would not hesitate
    To consider an alternate source.

"All the stud has to do is possess blood that's blue
    And be blind and unable to smell,
And then never aspire to want anything higher,
    And bingo! A match made in Hell!"

NEBULOUS IN LOVE

Said Pragmaticus, "Grand! We'll go combing the land
    Where we'll find guys like that by the dozens
In their little thatched huts with their thumbs in their butts,
    'Cause their mothers all married their cousins!

"But for now, leave it lay (*Time is leaping away*)!
    We have got to get moving, and fast.
Here's the gist of my plan to put you in the van
    In the race for my sister, at last.

"Now tonight, at the fling, here's how we'll do our thing
    When the party has barely begun,
Long before it's revealed that a deal has been sealed
    To Join Hunkus and Ampla as one.

"We will move really quick before Hunk smells a trick,
    And we'll switch Ampla dear for a ringer
Who'll string Hunkus along with a sweet, sexy song
    While she makes him believe he's a swinger.

"She will say her desire has consumed her with fire:
    She can't wait till they're formally wed;
Then she'll rip off her clothes and get down, toes to toes,
    Then and there with the bricks for a bed.

LeRoy Carl Blake

"Hunkus thinks he's so cool, but to say he's no fool
    Would be stretching the point a bit thin;
Thinking Ampla is asking to start multitasking,
    He will let his own deeds do him in!"

Then, Pragmaticus' smile underscoring his guile,
    He let go with his ultimate zinger:
With a lift of his head he triumphantly said,
    "We'll have Flatula playing the ringer!

"I will write to her, saying, I'm hoping and praying
    There's warmth in her heart for me still,
And I'll meet her tonight at the head of the flight
    Leading down from the Palatine Hill.

"Then, by Jupiter's knees, I must get me some Zs
    Before facing that orgy tonight;
So, if there's no loose end to which we must attend,
    I will rapidly fade out of sight."

Then Pragmaticus wrote his sly, masterful note,
    Filled with charming – though false-hearted – prose,
While young Nebulous said, "Um, there *is* a loose thread
    Of which I'd sort of like to dispose."

NEBULOUS IN LOVE

"Shoot," Pragmaticus said, "And then I'm off to bed!"
      And he gave his manservant the note,
With a word to make speed in promoting the deed
      That would keep the promoters afloat.

"Well, um," Nebulous said, "Getting Flatula wed
      Isn't all I've been trying to do;
The er, biggie is, I have to Shanghai some guy
      So Coita can get married, too."

"So Coita can . . . *what*? My god, what kind of nut
      Would take on such a hopeless endeavor?
You won't find such a man even if you could plan
      On the might of Minerva forever!

"And besides all that, who said it has to be you
      Who comes up with a Jack for each Jill?
If she needs a good man, well, it's catch as catch can;
      Let her find whom she can where she will."

"Were it only that easy," sighed Nebulous, queasy
      That now his friend might get upset,
"But that's Spectra's condition: I find a patrician
      Who's not heard of Coita yet."

LeRoy Carl Blake

"What has Spectra to do with Coita and you?"
      Asked Pragmaticus, fully awake;
"And what's this 'condition' that sounds like a mission
      To get someone hitched to that flake?

"Even you have to know that Coita's trousseau
      Will be only a comb and a wig;
What the hell will you do when she takes on the zoo
      And her husband decides to renege?"

"First of all, this 'condition' puts me in position,"
      Said Nebulous, hating the sight
Of his buddy dumbfounded at hearing propounded
      His latest impossible plight,

"To acquire all the cash that I'll need in my stash
      To confirm I'm no peasant in pawn,
So your dad will agree to wed Ampla to me
      When that idiot soldier is gone."

"You're as clear as a brick under mud an inch thick,"
      Said Pragmaticus, shaking his head.
"If I'm not overbold, why do *you* get some gold
      Out of Spectra if Coita's wed?"

NEBULOUS IN LOVE

"I'll explain it again," answered Nebulous then,
      Thinking maybe his friend wasn't quite
All as quick as he'd thought, for he certainly ought
      To have figured it out, were he bright.

"You know Spectra's a dame who's accustomed to fame:
      There's none better who knows how to bear it,
But she's lonely as hell in her big citadel
      With just ditzy Coita to share it.

"But Coita was made by the gods to get laid
      Ev'ry hour on the hour and then more,
And she drives Spectra nuts with no ifs, ands or buts,
      With her caricature of a whore.

"So, now, Spectra has said she'll agree to be wed,
      But that I must effect this attrition:
Get Coita a spouse and moved out of the house
      In accord with her lofty 'condition.'"

"You mean Spectra will *marry?*" Pragmaticus, wary,
      Said, "What in the hell did you do
To wind up with the chore of unloading her whore . . .
      Unless Spectra is marrying *you?*"

LeRoy Carl Blake

"Oh, yes, Spectra will wed, as I've already said,
    Though the prospective groom isn't me.
Just as soon as I get her kid sister all set,
    You may call me her stepson-to-be."

As Pragmaticus' jaw headed south in his awe,
    He imagined old Virtuous' verve
Asking Spectra to wed and to Nebulous said,
    "I'm surprised that he got up the nerve!"

"No, you've got it all wrong: I'm not beating a gong
    To keep Father from getting his due,
But my problem, in sooth – if you must know the truth –
    Is, he knows less of Spectra than you.

"Yeah, that's right. It's the height of my three-decker plight –
    After Hunk and Coita-the-tart –
That I haven't disclosed to my dad he proposed,
    Let alone to the bane of his heart."

"*What's this madness I'm hearing?*" Pragmaticus, fearing
    What else his old friend might admit,
Put his hands to his head: "Just a minute," he said.
    "Now, too much is enough, and *I quit!*

NEBULOUS IN LOVE

"Yesterday we agreed we should quickly proceed
      With a plan to get rid of your rival,
Since if I could help you I'd be helping me, too –
      A mere case of my mortal survival –

"And we drew up a deal that will virtually seal
      Hunkus' fate for today and hereafter,
Leaving Ampla to you and untying me, too,
      For a life filled with sunshine and laughter.

"Now you walk up and say, 'that's terrific, but hey,
      I am sort of in need of this mate
For Coita, the tart, or her sister won't start
      To consider a nuptial date;'

"In addition to which there's another slight hitch
      Which I notice you didn't quite mention:
Your old man is betrothed to a woman he loathed,
      Which is slightly apart from convention.

"And if that weren't enough to make smooth waters rough,
      Now you say that your dad doesn't know
He's engaged to be wed. Is he soft in the head?
      As I mentioned, pal, I gotta go."

LeRoy Carl Blake

"Okay!" Nebulous cried. "I was fit to be tied!
    Father sent me to ask her to wed;
I just couldn't commit, so I changed things a bit
    And proposed for my father instead.

"So, before you bolt, wait! Don't forget you've a date
    With the Fountain of Fragrance tonight;
All the good that you'll do will rub off on you, too,
    If you stay and go on with the fight.

"Prag, I need you tonight, to be witty and bright
    And prevail on that scent-laden elf
To put on a charade that will hotly persuade
    Noble Hunkus to bugger himself.

"So I'm begging you, stay! Please don't get blown away
    By the Gordian Knot of my life,
For tonight, if I fail, you will never prevail
    And foul Flatula will *be your wife!*"

Now Pragmaticus, stirred by the words that he heard
    From this youthful and bold paragon,
Stood and swore to his friend, "I will stick to the end!
    You can count on my help from now on!"

NEBULOUS IN LOVE

"Welcome back to the fight! Let us drink to tonight,"
      Toasted Nebulous, raising a cup
Of cheap Ludicrous wine which he thought was just fine,
      Though Pragmaticus nearly threw up.

"Now, all we have to do is to carry on through
      And make Ampla my sweet, blushing bride,
Then I'll tell Father dear, being candid and clear,
      With respect to dear Spectra, I lied.

"But Coita, of course, is a runaway horse
      Of a different color indeed,
And if I don't ensure a quick marriage for her
      I'll get thrown by that stampeding steed.

"Which is how we get back to my singular lack
      Of a suitable jerk for the job,
And why I need your brain to get Chastity's Bane
      Irrevocably tied to some slob."

But Pragmaticus knew there was no slob in view,
      And he bloody well couldn't invent one;
And as far as that goes, he could hardly propose
      To walk down to the Forum and rent one.

At the same time, however, Pragmaticus' clever,
    Bold wit didn't give up the ship:
He just thought for a minute, his heart and soul in it,
    And said, "Keep a stiff upper lip!

"There'll be plenty of studs among all the young bloods,
    So with luck we'll be able to find
At least one hungry gent so in hock for the rent
    He'll say yes to get out of his bind.

"But we'll keep him at bay – strictly out of the hay –
    Or he'll see how she's way oversexed,
And he may get a fright somewhere deep in the night
    When she casually hollers out, 'Next!'

"Then, I think, as they say, we can call it a day
    Till tonight when we romp with our neighbors;
And, our cunning completed, we'll stand undefeated
    Like Hercules after his labors."

"Until later tonight!" called his friend in his flight
    Toward his home and a bed of his own,
In a similar scene to his own fixed routine,
    Leaving Nebulous standing alone.

NEBULOUS IN LOVE

"I'll be free as a dove and I'll marry my love,
      As I knew I would do all along!"
Shouted Nebulous, sure that his goal was secure.
      "I mean, what in the world could go wrong?"

CHAPTER NINE

"This is different, all right," smirked our lad at the sight
    Of the walk leading up to the gate
Of the famed Chez Monyeux and the Celt's big to-do,
    To which father and son were both late.

"I have never before seen a house with its door
    At the end of its own private lane,
And with all of these quarters for lackeys and porters
    That line it, I think it's insane."

With that crude observation on flawed habitation,
    The pair hurried up the short run
'Twixt the blank-windowed rooms of the lackeys and grooms
    Set aglow by the far-setting sun.

All stood vacant and still in the gathering chill,
    For their occupants bent to the chore
Of cuisine preparation and mood augmentation
    While Phallus met guests at the door.

NEBULOUS IN LOVE

At the end, they went through with the last dawdling few
    To a pompously proud peristyle,
Where the sire of the bride – the groom's sire at his side –
    Greeted stragglers and shared Phallus' smile.

But the smiles disappeared – which was eerily weird –
    When the trio saw Nebulous there;
Phallus stayed quite polite; Gorgeosus took fright;
    But Vexatious commanded, "Beware!"

And, instilling pure dread in poor Virtuous, said,
    "Look, you sorry excuse for a peer,
If your kid starts a fight at this orgy tonight
    You'll be banned from the Senate, you hear?"

"He'll be safe as a saint," answered Virtuous, faint,
    As Vexatious' words rattled his ears,
Because Grievous Vexatious, renowned as loquacious,
    Had roundly ignored him for years.

"But the issue is dead," quickly Virtuous said
    As he shoved his young scion inside.
"He's inured to the fact that the Hunk's a class act
    Who will cherish his blushing new bride."

LeRoy Carl Blake

And as father and son, trying hard not to run,
        Were each handed a cup (of real glass!)
They observed that the aisle of the broad peristyle
        Was awash in a sea of old brass.

"I would say this suggests," said the father, as guests
        Shuffled past toward the atrium door,
"Of a hint that consists of the bond that exists
        'Twixt our host and our brave Emperor."

"Do you mean," asked the son, trying not to make fun
        Of the relics that lined all the walls,
"All these helmets and swords once belonged to the hordes
        Of the Northerners known as the Gauls?"

"They whom Phallus betrayed in an infamous raid,"
        Said his father, "for which he was made
A Praefectus, by which He's become very rich
        From the booty in which he was paid."

The pair tried to keep pace as they strode through the place
        With the mob in its feverish flow
From the stone peristyle to the rich, lustrous tile
        Of the atrium, warmly aglow.

NEBULOUS IN LOVE

"This is rich as whipped cream! It makes Sleazum's place seem
        Like a street peddler's cart in some square,"
Allowed Nebulous while they traversed the defile
        Taking stock of the luxuries there.

As they turned at the end – the quadrangular trend
        Of the atrium bore to the right –
Gaping Nebulous swore the great tablinum door
        Was the priciest treasure in sight:

"It's all ivory and wood!" He exclaimed as they stood
        And examined the portal wide-eyed;
"If he spent this much dough on that door, just for show,
        Then imagine the stuff that's inside!"

When they rounded the cool, sparkling atrium pool
        And were facing, again, the front door,
Our intrepid young lad slipped away from his dad
        And began, on his own, to explore.

And, while keeping an eye on the crowd passing by
        To avoid premature confrontation
Between Spectra and Dad – which could only be bad –
        Until Dad knew the whole situation,

LeRoy Carl Blake

He had thought it propitious to be surreptitious
    In finding his partner in crime,
For, with clear lack of vision they'd made no provision
    For where they would meet, or what time.

Thus, while Nebulous searched ev'ry face as he lurched
    Through the mob for Pragmaticus' grin,
By the happiest chance of a lateral glance
    He spied Ampla, who seemed in a spin.

Through the elegant door of a room, the decor
    Of which followed the latest French rage;
She looked très debonnaire in a new "chaise-longue" chair
    In the middle of friends her own age.

But it didn't take long to tell something was wrong
    By the bored look that everyone wore,
So he entered the room to see why all the gloom,
    And found Hunkus was holding the floor:

"....And be certain that *I*, forging in thigh to thigh,
    Thrust repeatedly into the action,
Never stopping until, with my soldierly skill,
    I achieved absolute satisfaction.

NEBULOUS IN LOVE

But, as Nebulous saw, the crowd seemed to withdraw
      More and more from the on-going drone;
So he backed through the door where he'd come in before,
      Leaving Hunkus to drone on his own.

But the one thing he knew as our hero withdrew,
      By the look on his cherished one's face,
Was that Hunkus had gone from "Don Juan" to "Dear John,"
      And that *he* was now back in the race.

Now he had to be quick with Pragmaticus' trick,
      Since his irons were all in the fire,
Or forever be left of his true love bereft
      If he blew it this close to the wire.

So he gave it his best, quickly scanning each guest
      For Pragmaticus' give-away grin,
When a bolt from the blue rocked his cozy canoe:
      Ye gods! Flatula won't be let in!

To a party this grand, for bestowing the hand
      Of a lady of Ampla's high station,
No mere tradesperson clod – or his daughter, by god!--
      Could dare hope for a stray invitation.

LeRoy Carl Blake

So he made up his mind that his friend was resigned
        To await him outside the chateau,
But on turning to leave someone's hand touched his sleeve,
        And Pragmaticus grinned his "hello."

"Am I glad to see you!" blurted Nebulous, who
        Looked surprised as he sniffed at the air,
"But. . .but where is that pearl of an odious girl
        Whom you promised to meet at the stair?"

"The good lady in question – at my kind suggestion –"
        Pragmaticus answered his chum,
"Waits for Hunk to come play by the main entrance way
        In a room called a cubiculum."

"As Pragmaticus deems, the gods act, so it seems,"
        Bubbled Nebulous, happy anew.
"I should learn to believe in what you can achieve!
        And now here's what we quickly must do:

"First, we act on our plan just as fast as we can,
        While dear Flatula's primed for the spoof,
For with her as time passes the mixture of gasses
        Might blow the cubiculum roof.

NEBULOUS IN LOVE

"Did you cover her head with a veil of bright red
        And make sure that her back's to the door,
So there's no way our swinger will know she's a ringer
        Till after he's gone for the score?"

"Hey, she's raring to go," said Pragmaticus, "though
        There's a hole in our plans for all that:
We've no witness to swear that Hunk even was there,
        Let alone that they went to the mat."

But then Nebulous smiled like a mischievous child
        And he nodded aside toward the room
Where his friend's sister sat, her expression as flat
        As the drone of her soon-to-be groom,

And he said, "Why not her? You must surely concur
        That the word of the 'woman aggrieved'
And the word of her brother, along with the other
        Young lady will most be believed."

He began to unveil his whole plan in detail,
        When a blaring of trumpets burst in
To the atrium mall from the peristyle hall
        Followed close by the god-awful din

LeRoy Carl Blake

Of a lot of guys drumming to jazz up the coming
    Of one too exalted to mention:
It was Feckless Despoticus, Sovereign Eroticus,
    Lapping up all the attention.

"There's no time to explain," explained Nebulous, fain
    To use Feckless' to-do as a cover,
"Just wait here by the door while I go to the fore
    With the trick that will win back my lover."

So, Pragmaticus did as young Nebulous bid,
    And stood ready to help stay the course;
Meanwhile, Nebulous ran the first step of their plan
    To abolish the quadruple force

Of (one) Hunk's petty greed and (two) Grievous' deep need
    For more power to add to his fame,
(Three) Phallus' fixation on cohabitation
    And (four) Sleaze's lust for a name.

Again Nebulous bore through the half-opened door
    After dodging the honking and drumming,
And was truly amazed to find Hunkus unfazed,
    And his monologue truly benumbing.

NEBULOUS IN LOVE

"Ahem, Hunkus," he said, ever forging ahead,
    "We're enthralled by your brave derring-do,
But – although it sounds rude – I must beg to intrude
    On your act for a minute or two."

Then, before Hunkus knew his big moment was through,
    He heard Nebulous say, "Here's the poop:
They've invented a game and some guy drew my name
    To come give everybody the scoop.

"So the first thing I'll do, is present all of you
    With a veil – well, for all of the girls –
And you'll each get to choose from a bunch of bright hues
    The best color to cover your curls."

And he walked through the crowd as they tittered aloud,
    Draping veils on the girls to their joy,
While he hid in his hand the bright red one he planned
    For his sweetheart to wear as a ploy.

And then, drawing quite near, he breathed, "Ampla, my dear,
    You have always looked stunning in red."
Then he helped her to don the bright crimson chiffon
    Like the one around Flatula's head.

LeROY CARL BLAKE

And, contriving to sneak a quick, recondite peek
      To make sure that the Hunk was aware
Of the raiment she wore, he made haste for the door
      And maneuvered himself out of there.

Once again in the hall by the atrium wall
      Where his ally, Pragmaticus, waited,
He reported, in brief, with a sigh of relief,
      That the bear trap was finally baited.

"Now it's up to you, chum," he said, jerking his thumb
      Toward the room in which Ampla still sat.
"As her dutiful brother, announce that your mother
      Would speak to her *inter se, stat!*

"Then, when Ampla's sprung free you can send her to me:
      I'll be near the front gate, with a view
Of the dark little room where she'll witness her groom
      Come to pitch Fragrant Flatula woo."

After that parting shot he was off at a trot,
      And Pragmaticus picked up his cue:
He went in to the girl with the ruby-red swirl
      'Round her head and said, "Mother wants *you*."

NEBULOUS IN LOVE

Gently taking her hand he remained in command
    As required in that long-ago day,
And then told her the score on their way to the door,
    Where she laughed before skipping away.

And as soon as she'd parted Pragmaticus started
    To soften up 'Hunkus-the-god,'
And laughed, "Hunk, you bad boy, Ampla's just being *coy*,
    And she wants me to bring her your bod."

"If your sister commands, I will tear, with these hands,
    Ev'ry obstacle 'twixt her and me
From the face of the earth!" bellowed Hunk without mirth
    Just to prove he was brave as can be.

"Put your troops to the trail! Let your captains set sail!
    They'll not live to see sunset this day!
I will smash every skull and capsize every hull
    Of whatever fool gets in my way!

"If fair Ampla's sweet calls from the depths of these halls
    Are for Hunkus to be with his bride,
Though the foe be ten score I will wade through the gore
    Of their fallen to go to her side.

LeRoy Carl Blake

"So make haste! Clear the way! I fear no man today,
      Though the beat of your drums reach the sky;
For the carnage that's wrought by my sword will be bought
      With the blood of the thousands who die!"

"Well um, yes. I can see you do seem to agree
      That a chat with my Sis would be nice;
It must thrill her no end that you'd kill, maim, and rend
      When a stroll down the hall would suffice."

So, the would-be new brothers departed the others
      And disappeared into the night;
Both men turned at the wall in the atrium hall;
      Hunkus, though, made a sharp column right.

When they reached the front aisle of the great peristyle
      And the entrance to grand Chez Monyeux,
The reception, at last, for His Highness had passed
      And the crowds had abandoned it, too.

So, they crept, keeping low, by the tombs-in-a-row,
      Where Pragmaticus played hide and seek
With the scarf of bright red around Flatula's head,
      Though he found her, at last, by her reek.

NEBULOUS IN LOVE

There, he saw through the gloom of a small-windowed room
    The red veil she submissively wore,
And without more to-do he bid Hunk toodle-oo
    And departed the little room's door.

"Psst! Hey, Prag, over here," His friend rasped in his ear
    From the flickering shadows at play
On the polished stone wall where his face disclosed all
    The rough moonlight would let him display.

"Where has Ampla-dear gone?" whispered Nebulous, drawn
    To Pragmaticus' side in the night;
"Didn't we just agree that she'd be here with me
    Before you two guys hove into sight?"

"But I sent her, I swear on Delicia's fair hair!"
    Croaked Pragmaticus, almost out loud,
"And if she isn't here, then I tremble with fear
    Knowing Phallus is loose in this crowd."

"Then it's clear I must go," whispered Nebulous, "though
    It were better to stay here and witness
The decline of the Hunk when that arrogant punk
    Gets to test his olfactory fitness."

LeRoy Carl Blake

"Hey, I'm coming with *you*," Said Pragmaticus, who,
    Having lured Hunkus into the room,
Heard the drone of Hunk's words like the hum of small birds,
    And knew Fame had won out over Fume.

"Because all that's left here," He went on, "is the fear
    Cupid's arrow may stray from its course;
If that's Cupid's intent, the young lady will vent
    Enough love to blow Hunk off a horse."

Whispered Nebulous, "So! To the rescue! Let's go!
    We must find out what Phallus has wrought,
And must find out before these two birds hit the floor:
    Without witnesses all is for naught!"

As they hurried away they heard Hunk holding sway,
    And Pragmaticus said to his pal,
"If she cuts through his flak by the time we get back,
    She's a very determined young gal."

"Let's split up at the door," answered Nebulous, sore
    As he watched all his plans come unknit,
And a little more scared for how Ampla had fared
    Than he'd care to believe or admit.

NEBULOUS IN LOVE

"Hurry up the left aisle of the grand peristyle,
      And I'll make a quick sweep of the right,
And together we'll march through the atrium's arch
      And check out every room within sight.

"And if we cannot trace the world's loveliest face
      Anywhere in this stack of cold stones,
May the Celt go unspared from the wrath I'm prepared
      To call down on his lecherous bones!"

And what Nebulous knew in his heart was all true!
      Their fat host *was* the sole inspiration
Of his love's disappearance through deft interference,
      Preempting her sweet assignation.

For, as fair Ampla flew to her sweet rendezvous
      In the arms of her writer of odes,
The old Celt had been pried from The Emperor's side
      By the lever of patronage toads.

So, it happened when she floated toward him that he,
      Quickly spotting her radiant glow,
Draped avuncular grace on his horny old face,
      And with warm, friendly greetings, bowed low.

"Ah, my beautiful child," the Praefectus had smiled,
    "What a pleasure to see you tonight
In your rush, I presume, to the side of your groom
    In whose triumphs we take such delight.

"But come hither, I pray, just a few steps away,
    For a moment and then you may go;
In the name of my love for your father, whereof
    I've a small wedding gift to bestow."

"Oh, your lordship!" said she, "You've a trinket for *me*?"
    And she stopped for the old plutocrat.
"There is naught I can say, as I skip on my way,
    To a generous offer like that.

"For as you wisely guessed I am really quite pressed
    To consort with my fiancé, whither
I am sure you can see there's no option for me
    To come hither before I go thither."

"I do see, ma cherie," said the Celt tenderly,
    Concern filling his velvety voice,
"But the diamonds I bring are too huge for a ring,
    So you simply must come make a choice

NEBULOUS IN LOVE

"From the trove of my treasure awaiting your pleasure
    Just seconds from this very spot,
Where I've buckets of gems, a few rare diadems,
    And more gold than a rainbow's old pot

"From Barbarian stores in the far northern wars
    Throughout Gaul-At-The-Top-Of-The-Boot
Where I fought with the best and outsmarted the rest
    For the lion's fat share of the loot.

"So, perhaps a nice chalice from old Uncle Phallus,
    Encrusted with diamonds and pearls,
Or a nice solitaire? Or, for all that, *a pair*
    For your ears 'neath those beautiful curls."

"You mean . . . *diamonds?*" She said. Now all other thoughts fled,
    And she halted without thinking twice:
For though diamonds were new, she had seen one or two
    And their splendor was more than just "nice."

So, her hand on his arm, feeling safe from all harm
    With this generous family friend,
She went through the carved door to the tablinum's core
    When they got to the atrium's end.

LeRoy Carl Blake

There were ebony tables and drapes made of sables;
    Triclinium lounges of silk;
And a shelf by the door with scrolled books by the score,
    All the creamy, rich color of milk.

The rare lamps were of gold, and looked foreign and old,
    And the floors were of inlaid parquet;
And the glint from the Gaul's alabaster-white walls
    That surrounded the girl told her, "STAY!"

"Here life's garden is spacious, enlightened and gracious;
    The woman within feels her worth;
Let your spirit unfold to the luster of gold,
    And the beautiful things of the Earth:

"Be transported tonight on a Heaven-sent flight
    From the world of the callous mundane
To the towering height of the Temple of Light
    In its rarified, heady domain.

"Be the true connoisseur! In your nimbus of myrrh,
    Let the priceless and rare overflow;
Make yourself feel at home with the riches of Rome
    As you hasten to *let yourself go!*

NEBULOUS IN LOVE

"I am moved," Phallus said, looking tense but well-fed,
    "That you honor this room with your presence;
You're my very first guest (Well, the first to be dressed)
    If you discount the goat and some peasants

"To come share with affection my own predilection
    For marvelous objects of art,
Whose more feminine features, alone among creatures,
    Make love to the strings of my heart."

"Oh, I do share your view," she agreed. "They outdo
    Almost anything else you can name,
And especially the ones with those bright little suns
    That dissolve their blue centers in flame."

"Ah, to live life surrounded by beauty unbounded!"
    Cried Phallus. "Each day I must see
Fresh, young, succulent treasures whose happiness measures
    Their talents at pleasuring *me*.

"And my gift, in return for such carnal concern,
    Is to honor each artist – it's true!
With a gem of my own for which I've become known;
    My renown has escaped very few."

"And the pleasure of giving that makes life worth living,"
    The lass wanted Phallus to know,
"Is increased with the size of the fiery prize
    The bestower is wont to bestow."

Phallus oozed, "You're so wise to disdain compromise:
    One should never place any constraints
On one's pleasure at all – somehow, one size fits all –
    Anyway, I have had no complaints."

"Oh, you marvelous man," the fair maiden began,
    "When I think of your offer to share
Such a treasure with me I can readily see
    You're a big, overgrown teddy bear!

"Your stupendous largesse just for my happiness
    Touches deeply my pure maiden's heart,
But, if I may be bold, when will you let me hold
    Nature's own perfect object of art?"

Phallus' subtle reaction of clear satisfaction
    With how things were going was shown
When he bowed to the knee and said, "Just follow me."
    In a soothing, mellifluous tone.

NEBULOUS IN LOVE

He then strolled through the works he had garnered as perks –
    Tons of dust-catching old merchandise –
Till he came to a door never opened before
    In the presence of anyone's eyes.

He then beckoned her there where a dark, narrow stair
    Was revealed in the tablinum's glow,
To descend from the light down a secretive flight
    To a hidden apartment below.

"Gee, it's spooky down here," echoed Ampla's high, clear
    Maiden's voice in the relative gloom
As Erectus came after with deep, muted laughter,
    And lighted a lamp in the room.

"Not to worry, my dear, where there's light, there is cheer,"
    The Praefectus encouraged his charge.
"Be it ever so humble there's room for a tumble,
    Though plainly it's not very large."

"Oh, a *bed*room," she cried, like a true blushing bride
    On her nuptial night at the Ritz,
"It's so frightfully dear, but how come we're down *here*?
    You think maybe we're in for a Blitz?"

LeRoy Carl Blake

"This small room, as you see, is known only to me,"
      Phallus smiled as an uncle would smile,
"And I come here to sleep because here's where I keep
      All the best stuff I've stashed in my pile."

And so saying, he stood by a chest of old wood
      That bore gouges from many a fight;
When he opened the lid to expose what it hid,
      He heard Ampla's great gasp of delight:

"By the gods!" she exclaimed, as the gemstones, enflamed
      By the light of the lamp filled her eyes
And the sheen of pure gold that could stop a heart cold
      Nearly caused her untimely demise,

"I can't make a selection from such a collection!
      Oh, what am I ever to do?
In deciding what's best from your vast treasure chest,
      I shall have to depend upon you."

With a deepening smile Phallus listened the while
      Her frustration was laid on the line,
Then he told her, "It's true, I know just what to do."
      But his smile was no longer benign.

NEBULOUS IN LOVE

"My considered advice is that diamonds are nice
      To embody the flame in your heart,
But remember: the Muse begs you also to choose
      From Erato's vast bounty of art."

He then turned from his guest and bent over the chest
      To withdraw a huge garment of gold
Decorated with gems and fur trim at the hems,
      Which he hastened forthwith to unfold.

"Though this frock hardly screams of the stuff of which dreams
      Are evolved in a bride's lovely head,
You're not gonna *believe* what you, too, can achieve
      When you slip it on once you're in bed!

"It is called a 'pourdeux' – it accommodates two –
      And in lands where its use is in fashion
Those who wear it in bed on the night they are wed,
      The gods free from all limits to passion.

"Though I know your heart's set on the diamond you'll get,
      I will wager this house and its land
The most fabulous gift I could possibly lift
      From this chest I now hold in my hand.

LeROY CARL BLAKE

"Now, in Rome it's enough just to sleep in the buff,
    For we never have risen above it,
But your husband-to-be is well traveled, and he
    Will have heard of this garment and love it."

So, in spite of her doubt, the fair maiden reached out
    To caress the gold cloth with her finger,
And her instant surprise struck a light in her eyes
    As the touch of pure gold made her linger.

"Try it on," Phallus said from the edge of the bed –
    His deep voice had turned throaty and thin –
And he helped her to don the smooth, golden chiffon
    Which engulfed her from toenail to chin.

He then managed to croak, "You must feel the gold stroke
    Your free soul as it breathes from within,
But to set your soul free know that nothing must be
    'Twixt your soul and the gold but your skin."

So she loosened the sash on her gown with panache
    As she laid herself down on the bed
To slip out of her clothes and lie there in repose
    Wrapped in nothing but yards of gold thread.

NEBULOUS IN LOVE

Glancing back at the stair – *Was there somebody there?* –
    And then down at his gilded gazelle,
Phallus' palms became damp as he lowered the lamp
    Before laying himself down as well.

He had known from the start that his plan, although smart,
    Would be wrecked if he didn't move fast,
And his thought, as he lay with his catch of the day
    Was, how *much* time has already passed?

For by now, he was sure, she'd be missed, and some boor
    From upstairs would start snooping around,
And the question was how he could honor his vow
    Of sweet vengeance before they were found.

Well, he wasn't down here just to play "uncle dear!"
    No! The point of his vast preparation
Hadn't centered at all on the garment from Gaul,
    But in fact on its live demonstration.

So, be damned that he knew what Vexatious would do
    If he caught him down here with the maid!
He had sworn to repay an injustice today:
    What was due was about to be paid!

LeRoy Carl Blake

But for all his resolve he could not disinvolve
      His concern from what should have been fun,
And his mind stayed alert as he touched the gold skirt
      Of the girl who would soon be undone.

His eyes gathered her tresses down wanton caresses,
      Then poured down her molten gold curves
To her pink, naked feet on his white linen sheet,
      And the sight of her knotted his nerves.

A sharp noise overhead made him leap from the bed –
      He must have her before 'twas too late!
Well, he'd finish this dame or his cherished nickname
      Throughout Rome wasn't Peter the Great!

Phallus swiftly undressed and squeezed into the vest
      With the girl mesmerized by the gold,
(But she quickly came to, when she realized who
      The guy was who came in from the cold.)

Open-eyed with surprise, she was suddenly wise
      To her "uncle's" intentions at last,
Which is not to suggest that her foresight, at best,
      Showed an intellect rarely surpassed;

NEBULOUS IN LOVE

And she fought tooth and nail to get free of her jail
    And the blubbery, naked Praefectus,
For by now she had learned how the fat man had earned
    The name Phallus Toujourus Erectus.

A new sound rent the air as a rare Grecian pair
    Of wine amphorae crashed overhead
(Phallus *did* wish whoever did that had been clever
    Enough to just drink it, instead);

But he nipped his reactions to upstairs distractions
    And turned his attention once more
To the bare-bottomed girl he held trapped in the furl
    Of the golden-hued garment they wore.

Then, a scuffling of muffled footsteps, as they shuffled
    Above them like whispering tongues,
Made the Celt hesitate at sweet maidenhood's gate
    While Sweet Maidenhood screamed out her lungs.

And the racket she made must have launched a parade
    If the noise overhead was a clue,
So he turned toward the stair to see who might be there,
    And fell out of the goddamn pourdeux!

LeRoy Carl Blake

Now, imagine it thus: a girl raising a fuss
    Romped in naught but a kaftan in sum,
While the lord of the place wore surprise on his face,
    Which was more than he wore on his bum.

Pandemonium reigned overhead, unconstrained,
    Though the mob seemed to want for direction;
While our singular pair glued their eyes to the stair
    In their mutual fear of detection.

For if Ampla, the dear, were caught anywhere near
    A love bed with this fat laughingstock,
Her bright future was through, and the Praefectus knew
    He'd be thrown from the Tarpeian Rock.

What was that? A dim face loomed atop the staircase
    Leading down to the depths of the palace;
The maid shot up in shock, but not so her gold frock,
    And she wound up as naked as Phallus.

But the Celt made a stand, the lamp high in his hand,
    His voice shaking, betraying his fear:
"Who now dares to intrude!" He stood trembling there, nude,
    As the face slowly made itself clear.

NEBULOUS IN LOVE

It was Nebulous, cast as a hero at last!
    Bravely facing the fat, naked twit,
He had rescued his bird! Overhead, the crowd heard,

"Oh, Nebbie!"
    "Oh, Ampla!"
        "Oh, *shit!*"

CHAPTER TEN

As young Nebulous sped down the stairway that led
    To his girl and the randy roué,
Quick inspection assured that he was, in a word,
    Somewhat better appareled than they:

Dearest Ampla stood, Bare, in the little lamp's glare,
    Shielding all that she could from his eyes;
Though she tried with both arms, the demands of her charms
    Far exceeded her coverage supplies;

And the pale, pasty Gaul, looking shriveled and small
    By the light of the flickering flame,
Had deflated in air – which displayed his despair –
    With his bowed, bandy legs for a frame.

Like a shot, Ampla hied to young Nebulous' side
    Where she hid in the folds of his clothing,
For, as Nebulous guessed, he had caught them undressed,
    And he glared at the fat man in loathing.

NEBULOUS IN LOVE

His heart wanted to cheer, HE HAD SAVED AMPLA DEAR!
    But he also was filled with misdoubt,
When he saw that the room, like a chamber of doom,
    Boasted only one way to get out.

While our hero debated, the Celt hadn't waited:
    He snatched up the huge golden vest,
Grabbed her gown from the floor, popped a wee, secret door,
    And was *gone* with her gown and the chest.

Now the voices grew loud as the overhead crowd,
    Who had followed the screams to the stair,
Began trickling down to emerge with a frown
    When they saw what awaited them there.

In the room, they'd attest, was their host's honored guest
    With a man – neither brother nor sire –
And the hullabaloo was attributed to
    Their dissimilar states of attire.

"Who are you!" snapped a man in the fore of the van
    Of the gapers who stood on the stairs,
"What in hell have you done to the daughter of one
    Of our most senior men of affairs?"

LeROY CARL BLAKE

Then a chorus of, "Rape!" and, "Don't let him escape!"
    Bounded forth from the echoing walls,
To explode up the stair to the tablinum where
    It was picked up and spread down the halls

To that little front room yet beclouded in gloom
    Where the soldier expounded his deeds:
Hunkus still hadn't let fragrant Flatula get
    A small word in regarding her needs.

"And of course it was I who cried, 'Lads, do or die!'
    As I rallied the garrison's pride,
And the soldiers I led through the open soon bled;
    For I *did* while they followed and died!

"And you'll simply be floored by the points that I scored,"
    He was modestly going to add,
"Among all of those Greeks who love manly physiques,"
    When he heard someone yell, "Hang the cad!"

"Someone's hanging a cad?" *This can only be bad!*
    Hunk was dallying too far away,
For the shouts, he conceded, were proof he was needed
    (As always) to come save the day.

NEBULOUS IN LOVE

"I must fly, Ampla dear." he commanded: "Wait here
    While I hasten to answer the call.
I'll return in a trice, when I've made it all nice,
    With more stories to keep you in thrall.

But poor Flatula wept as the man fairly leapt
    From the room like a five year old boy
Whose persona rebelled as if he were compelled
    To stay put in one place with one toy.

As she got to her feet and walked out to the street
    She discarded the bright, crimson veil:
She had failed to attract – with the deck clearly stacked –
    An available, suitable male.

But the Hunk didn't care. He was walking on air
    As he followed the noise to ground zero,
And mere girls didn't play a big role anyway
    In this business of being a hero.

At the tablinum door, sacrosanct to the core
    And off limits to all but the Gaul,
Hunkus screeched to a halt; could his eyes be at fault?
    All the guests were *inside* the grand hall.

LeROY CARL BLAKE

"Move your arses!" he cried, shoving gawkers aside
      As he strode through the room to the stair
Which, it needn't be said – even Hunk got the thread –
      Was the focus of everyone there.

Then he held up his palm to bring silence and calm,
      And demanded, "What's this all about?
As good Romans you knew that this room was taboo,
      So now everyone get the hell out!"

But a Senator, clad in a toga, who had
      Little reason to fear Hunkus' clout
Stepped before him and said, in a manner well bred,
      That which all but the Hunk figured out:

"Everybody, it seems, heard the terrible screams
      That came wave upon wave through the air;
So we followed them here where it's only too clear
      That the screamer was screaming down *there*."

Hunkus roared, "Never fear, Gorgeosus is here!"
      And he bellowed a soldierly shout
As he charged down the stair, bowling into the pair
      Whom the whole bloody flap was about.

NEBULOUS IN LOVE

(For some reason this act of superlative tact
      Always managed to dampen the mood
Of the ones who went *splat* after getting knocked flat
      By this Model of Just Rectitude.)

As the guests flailed about sorting arms and legs out,
      Not to mention their tangled up clothes,
Hunk was startled to learn he'd slammed into the stern
      Of the upstart he'd stretched by the nose.

He was still on the ground, sort of lying around,
      While he counted his toes and his teeth,
When the Hunk grabbed his arm and then viewed with alarm
      Who was lying around underneath.

"My, you're certainly fast," stammered Hunkus at last
      To his mortified, soon-to-be bride,
Who was bare from her hair all the way down to *there*
      And nowhere, thanks to Hunkus, to hide.

"It's a comfort to see you're so happy to be
      At my side that you followed me here,
But I'd still like to know how you got down below
      Before *I* got here, Ampla my dear.

LeROY CARL BLAKE

"Yes, there's something amiss at the center of this –
    I just can't let it ruin my day –
It's a small, nagging doubt . . . Ah! I figured it out:
    You have lost your red veil on the way."

"Only you would say that!" hapless Nebulous spat.
    "By the gods, you damn fool, are you blind?
She has nary a stitch on her tushy, for which
    Your concern is a little behind."

"Well, by Jupiter's might, little man, you are right!
    She *is* naked 'neath you in repose."
Whereupon, with dispatch, Hunk secured a firm latch
    Once again upon Nebulous' nose.

"Now you'd better explain why *you're* in the domain
    Of this cozy bed-chamber tonight
With my soon-to-be bride, dressed in naught but her hide,
    Whom you've given a terrible fright!"

With a snort of disdain Hunkus stood once again,
    Hauling Nebulous up from the floor,
And the poor fellow rose – he just followed his nose –
    To the heights he had been to before.

NEBULOUS IN LOVE

With our hero held thus in a three-fingered truss
    Like some verminous filth – only more so –
Hunkus sneered as he said, "She'll have your clothes instead!"
    And ripped Nebulous' robe from his torso.

Once assured his betrothed was again fully clothed –
    What the hell did she do with her gown?—
Hunkus strutted around the boudoir underground
    Making up to each one he'd knocked down:

"Beg your pardon, good sir, unless you are a 'her,'
    In which case its 'good madam,' I guess;
It's so hard to know who one is pandering to –
    I mean, really, you're all such a mess!

"I am happy to say this is your lucky day –
    Now, don't all kiss my sandals at once! –
You can be of good cheer: Noble Hunkus is here
    To save all of your hides from this dunce.

"For this knave that I hold by the nose has made bold
    To affront darling Ampla (my love),
For which deed he shall pay when I've hauled him away
    To Vexatious, who's waiting above."

LeRoy Carl Blake

As his words hit the air Hunkus turned with a flair
    In the manner becoming a star,
And with Nebulous fast in his grip as he passed,
    Glided grandly across the boudoir.

He arrived at the stair, which he mounted, and there,
    Waving Nebulous high in the breeze,
The one-man cavalcade of Hunk's private parade
    Crossed the holy of holies with ease.

At the back of the crowd (Where The Portal stood proud,
    Open now to the atrium hall)
Hunkus saw with delight Mars was smiling tonight,
    For outside stood the Hero of Gaul.

There, with laurels askew and sweat blocking his view
    Through his booze-laden, bleary-eyed grin,
Tottered Feckless Despoticus, sexpot eroticus,
    Drooling from each double chin.

And around him, a score of the sycophant corps
    Who were always wherever he'd be,
Which included, tonight, right up close and in tight,
    The first two of the Infamous Three:

NEBULOUS IN LOVE

First, Vexatious, of course, wore a face to enforce
>What he thought was the casual pose
Of a man of position (Above mere ambition)
>Whose cup of renown overflows;

Next was Georgeus – whose heir now approached from the stair –
>Who was running a close number two
In the race for the prize for superfluous size
>In the mass of one's gross revenue.

The third man of the three – he of Celt pedigree –
>For what reason no one had a clue,
Wasn't there at his post as the other men's host,
>And, in fact, wasn't *near* Chez Monyeux.

Hunkus' heart filled with pride with each confident stride
>Toward the god just outside the great door,
As the aim of his game with Vexatious became
>A new aim to lay claim to much more.

Thus he carefully laid the bold scene to be played
>In which he would receive (in his shyness)
Words in praise of his deed for a damsel in need,
>And he'd get them, what's more, from His Highness.

LeROY CARL BLAKE

Now, in fear of his wrath the mob cleared him a path
    When he strode toward the limelight, to share it,
Holding high in his hand by its olfactory gland
    Naked Villainy, clothed in its merit.

CHAPTER ELEVEN

"Why, how dare you to bring that vile, garmentless thing
    To be swung 'neath the Emperor's eyes!"
Gorgeosus exclaimed while his son, unashamed,
    Held the nose of his unadorned prize.

But Vexatious, whose plum the young Hunk had become,
    Saw him heading for Feckless instead,
And he cagily gauged he was being upstaged,
    So he stepped in between them and said:

"My good lad, I can see that you're looking for *me*
    With that creature from out of our past,
Who by now would be dead if I'd just used my head
    When you caught him the night before last!

"But we needn't frustrate noble Rome's head of state
    With the antics of one foolish kid;
Leave the matter with me and I'll happily see
    That he pays for whatever he did.

LeRoy Carl Blake

"You must let me explain," Hunkus sputtered in vain
    As Vexatious stood blocking his way
To the exquisite door, the bemused Emperor,
    And his dream of the jackpot that day.

"This young cad that I dangle came up with an angle
    Not one of us dreamed that he would:
For his plan was to rape Ampla dear and escape,
    But I saved her again ere he could!"

But the god had not heard, so he yelled every word:
    "I have saved my dear Ampla from *rape!*
Though this dastardly cad I hold prisoner had
    Tried to ravish the girl and escape!"

Now Vexatious went cold at the instant Hunk told
    Of the deed that had nearly occurred,
And though Hunk's monolog had the crowd all agog,
    The old Senator heard just one word.

"Rape *my* daughter?" he roared, like a bull that's been gored
    As the poet's feet churned in the air;
His bile started to rise and he glared at the eyes
    Of the lad who'd dared even to *dare.*

NEBULOUS IN LOVE

"You insufferable dunce! You were warned more than once
      To stay out of this family's affair;
Now, by Jupiter's wife, you will pay with your *life*
      For your crime against maids everywhere!

Then Vexatious left Hunk, who went into a funk
      When he failed to win royal attention,
And returned to the clown with the Cracker Jack crown
      To beseech his divine intervention:

"O Divinity, say that you'll make this dog pay,"
      The old Senator growled as he frowned
At poor Nebulous, who without much else to do,
      Was still casually hanging around.

"This good soldier, in fact, caught the cad in the act
      Of a wallow with young maidenhood,
And it's clear by the lack of a stitch on his back
      That he plainly was up to no good!

"It is bound to disgust all of Rome's upper crust
      That he blunders about in the buff,
And I share your outrage at his wanton rampage,
      And agree we must punish this stuff."

LeRoy Carl Blake

But the god, unimpressed, drained his cup and confessed,
    "How can *you* believe *I'd* be outraged?
Any fool can attest that he's properly dressed
    For the sport in which he was engaged."

Calmly having a stroke at his Emperor's joke,
    It was nonetheless clear to Vexatious
That he *must* keep his cool, for the man, though a fool,
    Was revered through his drool as sagacious.

With a laugh as robust as his hidden disgust,
    The old Senator tried one more time:
"Oh, you're *the* soul of wit *You insufferable twit!*
    But Your Highness *must* deal with this crime.

"So before you object, won't you kindly direct
    That your personal guard be dispatched
To pry loose that proboscis from yonder colossus,
    Along with the scoundrel attached?"

While he struggled to focus on Grievous' blurred locus
    To answer the Senator's plea,
The fat Emperor belched, and before it was squelched,
    Of his four loyal guards he'd felled three.

NEBULOUS IN LOVE

"Uh, with all due regard for your late bodyguard,
    At whose loss I am sure you're bereft,"
Tried Vexatious again, "Won't you see to it then,
    While you still have that one fellow left?"

"Absholooly, old son, rest assured 'twill be done!
    Am I not a Late Greader of Men?
Your command is my wish, though *you* look kinda swish;
    Um, what was it you wanted again?"

"I've suggested, brave sir, throw the blackguard in stir
    For the tears that his victim is shedding;
Have him locked up tonight! I'll be there at first light
    To arrange for his trial and beheading."

Then, to cut off the slob with the world's highest job
    And get on with the work of the day,
The old solon showed how merely raising one's brow
    Could work wonders if done the right way.

For his glance, unobserved by the guests, so unnerved
    The sole guard at the Emperor's rear
Who, by luck and location still stood at his station,
    He switched his allegiance in fear.

And, impaled on that fine, unmistakable sign
    That said, "Fail me and meet your demise,"
The young guard found the spunk to march up to the Hunk
    And demand to be given his prize.

Well now, Hunkus, of course, was as big as a horse,
    And although the young guardsman was too,
When the Hunk took his place with the guard face to face
    He looked roughly the size of Peru.

So the guard was refused, not to mention abused,
    With a straightforward, filthy assault
On his mother, whose habits, reminiscent of rabbits,
    The Hunk was reluctant to halt:

"Why, you unbidden son of a maiden unwon!
    You pathetic excuse for a man!
The Praetorian Guard's made of Army discards,
    As it has been since when it began!

"Who the hell do you think captured this little fink
    In flagrante delicto tonight?
Well, the trophy is mine, and I'm damned if I'll sign
    Over spoils to a *guard* and not fight!"

NEBULOUS IN LOVE

But, while Hunk kept a grip on the guardianship
      Of his hope for a ticket to fame,
It was clear that Vexatious, grown more disputatious,
      Was bored by his asinine claim:

"My dear fellow," said he, "We're all proud as can be
      To see what a fine hero you make;
Now that you've made your point, put your nose back in joint,
      Stop your pouting, and *give us a break!*"

Hunkus' fury was fanned by Vexatious' command;
      He would countenance no intervention!
But his fatherly kin grabbed his scrotum, wherein
      He just managed to gain his attention.

In a whisper he said, "Listen, Son, use your head!
      Don't go putting Vexatious to strife;
If you grouse the old man he could muck up your plan
      To make Ampla – his daughter – your wife."

Now, his father's decision to foster revision
      Of Hunkus' entrenched point of view
By the casual seizing of assets and squeezing
      Proved Daddy knew just what to do.

LeRoy Carl Blake

His eyes tearing in pain, Hunkus fought to contain
      A harmonic beyond human reach,
And from up on his toes he piped, "Jupiter knows,
      This is nothing my manuals teach!"

Gorgeosus, though small, kept the repartee ball –
      If you'll pardon the usage – in play:
"You may notice my grip isn't on scholarship,
      So who cares what your manuals say?"

With a twist so intense – a quick turn of events –
      That the Hunk was in fear for his life,
Gorgeosus said, "Son, give it up and be done
      While you're still of some use to a wife;

"For, if out of ambition you hold your position,
      You surely must know I will, too,
And before we are finished you'll be so diminished
      No maiden will *want* to wed you."

And so Hunkus gave in, seething livid chagrin
      At the loss of the glory he'd sought,
And he handed the nose, like the summer's last rose,
      To the guardsman he'd rather have fought.

NEBULOUS IN LOVE

But his mood was just shot! And, more likely than not,
    His own pater had ruined his day,
For his cheeks were still burning while Dad was returning
    Control of his swing to his sway.

"The vile fiend's been arrested!" Vexatious attested
    When Hunkus had finally passed
To the fist of the guard the bent beak of the bard
    So the solon could wrap up the past.

With stentorian thunder the Togated Wonder
    Declaimed to the guests loud and long
Till, his dewlap aquiver, his words shot a shiver
    Of moral resolve through the throng:

"Now, I ask all of you what you'd tell us to do
    With this treacherous, trespassing toff
Who was not only caught with his pants down, but thought
    He could wander around with them *off*?

"Who among you would see this vile creature set free
    To continue his rape (or to try)?
Or should "justice for all" be our rallying call,
    And condemn the young rounder to die?"

Thus, with catcalls and shouts all the guests thereabouts
    Who would follow wherever he led
Soon had fallen in line with Vexatious' design
    And were screaming for Nebulous' head.

But aside, in the gloom at the edge of the room,
    A lone senator stood at his place,
Where he watched, full of dread, as they yelled for the head
    Of his son, now in total disgrace.

"Oh, ye flesh of my flesh, why did you so enmesh
    All our dreams with your stupid affair?"
The old back-bencher wailed as again his hopes failed
    And he felt he would drown in despair.

With no fictive pretense at a vain social sense,
    He was openly shocked, and he reeled
At his sentence – *for life!* – to penurious strife
    Which the seizure of Nebulous sealed.

Though he covered his eyes, he could still hear the lies
    He had told himself day after day:
To pretend to the end his son didn't intend
    To take Ampla to wife come what may.

NEBULOUS IN LOVE

But, his bitter tears dried and the ache turned inside,
      He now shifted concern for *his* fate
To concern for his son, and what now could be done
      For his neck, if it wasn't too late.

For, though Nebulous strongly – and certainly wrongly –
      Inspired all his troubles this day,
Through the pain of his sorrow he knew that tomorrow
      He'd stand by his son come what may.

Having firmly resolved to get fully involved
      In preventing his offspring's demise,
He began to think out how to bring it about,
      And relaxed and uncovered his eyes.

But what leaped into view before each baby blue
      As he lowered his hands to his side
Brought another great shock to a man of his stock,
      And he stood like a rock, stupefied.

Standing there, with her hair swept aloft without care
      Above eyes that inspired abject terror,
It was Spectra, of course, who began her discourse:
      "Are you Ludicrous, Jupiter's error?"

LeRoy Carl Blake

"I am he." The man cringed, and his gut fairly twinged
      Like a lamb singled out for the slaughter,
As he inwardly raged at the gods who had staged
      Such ill timing by Hecate's daughter.

"Though I certainly know," she continued, as though
      He were used to her high-handed chatter,
"That your blood is as blue as the birds in the zoo,
      It's your Ludicrous actions that matter.

"For, although your great name is your ticket to fame,
      As it has been for hundreds of years,
It remained so because of no scandalous flaws
      In your Ludicrous Senate careers;

"But what happened tonight is the absolute height
      Of the lowest of low, sneaky deeds,
And I fear the new shame on your Ludicrous name
      Doesn't interface well with my needs.

"So, to be quite precise, it sure would have been nice
      To have Rome at my feet as your wife,
But with things as they are I'll get three times as far
      With you idiots out of my life.

NEBULOUS IN LOVE

"For, while I still aspire to blue blood, my desire
        To finance your ambition has flown;
Now your ill-disguised yearnings for indecent earnings
        Will have to await the next crone."

And with that, the old girl disappeared in a whirl
        As she strode to the door and walked out,
Leaving Virtuous there asking naught but thin air
        What in Saturn's name *that* was about.

But before he collected his wits and connected
        Her chiding with Nebulous' plot,
She looked back from the door across Phallus' fine floor
        And appended a last parting shot:

"Oh, and as for my sister, you needn't assist her
        In finding a suitor to wed;
I'll just buy her a man on the lay-away plan
        Who will promise to chain her in bed."

Now in hopeless confusion at Spectra's allusion
        To Coita's marriage, to wit:
She had said to forget it before she had set it;
        He gathered his toga and split.

LeRoy Carl Blake

But as Virtuous strode from Toujourus' abode
    In his rush to get out of the din,
He was feeling so low he had no care to know
    Who it was that he passed coming in.

Thus it was that the Sleaze gained admittance with ease
    To this bedlam of blue-blooded bores,
For, with Phallus gone missing his staff was dismissing
    Itself from security chores.

And the Sleaze was as mad as a hen who'd just had
    A surprise skinny-dip in the Tiber
As he shoved men aside in his unyielding stride
    To get past each Patrician imbiber.

Because Sleazum's prime goal, beyond all self-control,
    Was to corner the mighty Vexatious,
And throw right in his face, to his lasting disgrace,
    That his motives were purely rapacious.

Sleazum reached the great door with its carvings galore
    As a guard was removing the trash,
Which he swung by its nose to make sure that its toes
    Held no hope for a getaway dash,

NEBULOUS IN LOVE

And he stood, to the awe of the father-in-law
    He had tried to line up for his whelp,
And the near total shock to the rest of the flock
    In the sight of the god, to seek help.

"Lordly Feckless, I pray," He had started to say,
    "I have something Your Highness must know,
And I've come here tonight to put wrong matters right...."
    But then Grievous took over the show:

"That you've come here at all shows a fat lot of gall!"
    He injected, in fear for his life
That this merchant from Hell had decided to tell
    How he'd diddled the Emperor's wife.

"Just where is it you think you are standing, you *fink?*
    Who the hell let you into this place?
We're a blue-blooded crew, and we don't truck with *you!*
    Now get out or I'll rework your face."

"No! It's you who will pay for your folly this day,"
    Screamed the Sleaze in a hurried recap:
"When the god learns your son used my daughter *in fun*
    To lure Hunkus, there, into a trap.

"Yes, my Darling came crying that, though she was trying
    To meet all your high expectations,
Your son found her a room where yon soon-to-be groom
    Made a stab at improper relations."

"You mean Grievous and son have made improper fun
    Of a maiden?" the Emperor drooled.
"Why, then, Grievous, you ass, have your boy wed the lass –
    Just as soon as your temper has cooled."

Well now, Sleazum was beaming, but Grievous was *screaming*:
    "Divinity, how can this be?
You have heard but one side from a man who has lied,
    Yet you bring down your hand against *me*."

When Despoticus drank he just drank 'til he stank,
    And tonight he had drunk quite a lot:
"Don't dispute what I said, or I'll chop off your head!"
    Was the only reply Grievous got.

But the merchant, ecstatic, called Feckless "Socratic,"
    And couldn't let well enough rest;
He began mocking Grievous, who screamed at him, "Leave us!
    You flea-bitten, merchant class . . . *pest!*"

NEBULOUS IN LOVE

"Don't get touchy with me, or the god, here, will see
      That they wipe up the floor with your head,"
Chuckled Sleazum, "and, too, I could *still* say that you
      And Lascivia once went to bed."

The last crack must have tapped something deep: Grievous snapped,
      And he lunged for his tormenter's hide
With his bared snickersnee when a fresh set of three
      Palace Guards pinned his arms to his side.

"You would *dare* start a fight? It is *you* I'll indict!"
      Bellowed Feckless at hapless Vexatious;
"Guards, take him away to some place where he'll stay
      Until noon when he feels less pugnacious,

"And then call him to trial for his utterly vile
      And uncalled-for behavior tonight,
When I'll chop off his head to be certain he's dead
      And forever cast out of my sight!"

And so Grievous was taken, defeated and shaken,
      By guards with imperial clout
From the grandiose hall where the guests, all-in-all,
      Were now mumbling and milling about.

For the later it grew, from the guests' point of view,
> The more hungry they got, and more bored,
And with Phallus not there his staff just didn't care,
> For they served no one else but their lord.

So, throughout the great palace the shouts of "Where's Phallus?"
> Already were batting their ears
As the guests, still unfed, loudly threatened to shred
> Chez Monyeux into small souvenirs.

All but Hunkus, of course, the immutable force
> Whose persona was sundered and sore;
In a simpering snit with his sword he'd seen fit
> To hew down the great tablinum door.

And as bedlam increased joviality ceased
> When the goblets of wine had run dry,
For their host for the night was still nowhere in sight,
> And "*get* Phallus!" was now the great cry.

"The gods must have gone mad to let things get this bad!"
> Panted Virtuous, flat-out in flight,
As the dirge of dismay faded farther away
> Through the thundering thick of the night.

NEBULOUS IN LOVE

But he slowed to a trot when he found that he'd got
    Out of range of his pillaging peers,
And the clap of his feet on the dark, quiet street
    Seemed to echo his innermost fears:

Where had Nebulous gone? Could he last until dawn?
    And how *could* he have been such a fool?
Why did he go berserk and become such a jerk
    With the one girl he thought was so cool?

Was he already dead? If relieved of his head
    It would ransom Vexatious' tranquility,
And the absence of Phallus (with murderous malice?)
    Gave life to that new possibility.

He lurched through the dark he held fast to a spark
    Of faint hope that he'd not be too late,
And he cried to the gods not to go with the odds,
    But deliver his son from his fate.

Then, he saw it! Ahead was the flickering red
    Of a torch above scurrying feet
Where three men marched apace, and he leapt to the chase
    Toward the light, down the upper-class street.

CHAPTER TWELVE

From the Palatine Hill, down the stairway that still
    Linked the Forum with those up above,
Faithful Virtuous ran, the lamp still in the van,
    Filled with hope, and with fatherly love.

Then, abruptly, the flare reached the end of the stair
    And careened toward the little taverna
Where the supplicants stay when they go there to pray
    At the shrine near the pool of Juturna.

Out of breath, he drew near what he thought, from the rear,
    Was a three-person Guards retinue,
'Till he noticed the one who went in was his son,
    And the men under arms were but two.

"Hail Despoticus, Ho!" hollered Virtuous, though
    It is said he would later attest
A soft word would have got their attention and not
    Caused them both coronary arrest.

NEBULOUS IN LOVE

"Ah, good soldiers," he said, "I would fain lay my head
    In this comforting cottage's care;
Prithee say I can stay until first light of day
    When Juturna will call me to prayer?"

"Sure, if you ain't opposed to a black-and-blue-nosed
    Scrawny kid as the sole other guest,"
Said the Guard with the flare, who was very aware
    Of the rank of the man he addressed.

"Course, at dawn you should know how this thing's gonna go,"
    Said the other one, also impressed,
"When we do what we do to the kid, so that you
    Don't get splattered while you're gettin' dressed."

"When you do what you . . . *do?*" stammered Virtuous, who
    Had forgotten that Guards, by and large,
Were more practiced at lopping off heads than at chopping
    Up enemy troops in a charge.

"I shall try to avoid being thusly annoyed,"
    Was his faintingly feeble riposte
As he shakily groped through the door which he hoped
    Would reveal whom he longed to see most.

LeRoy Carl Blake

Thus, he entered the gloom of the stony cold room
    Filled with smoke from a guttering lamp
Insufficiently bright to give substantive light,
    And of less effect still on the damp.

"Oh, my boy! Are you there? this poor, god-bereft flare
    Stings my eyelids and beggars my sight;
If you're near, call my name! My ears won't need a flame
    To come join you and watch through this night."

Then, against the cold wall of the dungeon-like hall,
    Slumped in mortification and shame,
The old solon beheld youthful innocence felled,
    And he knelt as he whispered his name:

"Oh, dear Nebulous, lad! Know that nothing's so bad
    In the darkest of life's dark estates
But some good will result in which you can exult
    If you dwell in the smile of the Fates.

"And who else can be found of this good Roman ground
    Who could lay greater claim to that fame
Than a poet from birth who has known true love's worth
    And was willing to die for love's flame?

NEBULOUS IN LOVE

"Oh, be brave, my own son! though your world is undone,
    Just believe that your father is right:
The Weird Sisters have shown they love you as their own
    And will aid in your desperate fight.

"But you must understand that *the time is at hand* –
    For they vanish at first light of day –
It is *now* they elect whom they'll help or reject,
    And what price for their favors we'll pay.

"Quickly, now! Make a deal that at dawn they'll reveal
    As we rise from our nocturnal bed,
That their pleasure will be to set you, my son, free
    And to topple Vexatious instead."

But a feeling of doom filled the dark, clammy room
    When young Nebulous failed to reply,
And the Senator knew without further ado
    That at sunup his scion would die.

But he'd vowed he would stay by his side come what may,
    Through the pain the long hours would evoke,
And as dread crushed his mind with what daybreak would find,
    He was startled when Nebulous spoke:

LeRoy Carl Blake

"I am sorry, dear Dad, that the end is so sad
    When you strove for much better than this;
And it would have been, too, if I'd listened to you
    And not followed my ignorant bliss.

"You were always so kind that I just became blind
    To the need to *grow up* and get straight;
When the going got rough and you finally got tough,
    It was already eons too late.

"But who cares what the cause! I have crushed in the jaws
    Of my childishly self-centered life
All the things I desired because I was inspired
    To take Ampla Vexatious to wife.

"But now Ampla is gone, like a nymph with her faun
    To the bed of that fatuous bore,
Where you said she would go at least ten times or so!
    So, the girl of my dreams is no more.

"And that's not all I've done! As a true, faithful son
    I've ensured that the Ludicrous name
So respected for years by our blue-blooded peers,
    From now on will bring nothing but shame;

NEBULOUS IN LOVE

"Which means now you cannot hope to better your lot
      By a marriage to bolster your purse,
For the one thing you had was your name, and – too bad!
      Now your name, thanks to me, is your curse.

"But my coup of the day, proving far and away
      Selfish means bring about a bad end,
Wasn't staking my claim to destroying our name,
      But destroying my very best friend.

"For Pragmaticus now has to marry that *cow*
      And inherit a slow, living death
With a sulfurous brat of such qualities that
      She can giggle while stopping your breath.

"Now he's firmly impaled because Yours Truly failed
      To foresee all the rocks in the stream,
And proceeded to dash all our hopes in the crash
      Of my schoolboyish, scatterbrained scheme.

"Well, the scheme didn't work because I was a jerk,
      And it's no use to call on The Fates;
With what they think of me I'm quite certain that we
      Wouldn't even get overnight rates!"

LeRoy Carl Blake

Troubled Virtuous, then, who'd been thinking again,
    Jumped as though he'd been suddenly struck:
"As you spoke, I could see it is plainly *The Three*
    And not you who's behind our bad luck!"

Neither Hunkus, you see, nor the Sycophant Three
    Would be bothered with moves to proscribe
So unworthy a pair as myself and my heir,
    So, *The Fates* must be screwing our tribe!

Humbly, Virtuous said, "Though they fill me with dread,
    I will call them and beg for your life;
If they say you may live, here's my promise to give
    My consent to your choice for a wife."

The boy thought of the years when, ignored by his peers,
    His old father had waited in vain,
And as Virtuous prayed for his death to be stayed,
    Doleful Nebulous shared in his pain.

The hours drifted away toward the oncoming day
    When the whim of The Fates would be known,
And then, just before dawn, with all vanity gone,
    The condemned said some words of his own:

NEBULOUS IN LOVE

"Oh, my trusting old Dad! What a *bastard* you had!"
      And he shuddered with shame as he said:
"It was all up to me and I just would not see
      The great future you knew lay ahead.

"Now I go to my death, and with every last breath
      I regret that I didn't do more. . ."
He was going to add that he loved his old Dad,
      When he heard a Guard open the door.

CHAPTER THIRTEEN

The men leapt in surprise and with dim, burning eyes
    Swung their gaze as the door opened wide;
They sat stark staring still in the dark, smoky chill
    As a form, unrevealed, stepped inside.

"Hey! Is Nebulous here? Where's the main chandelier?
    I can't see a damn thing in this place!
And if breathing this smoke is some kind of a joke,
    Eighty-six it and cut to the chase!"

"It's Pragmaticus, Dad!" shouted Nebulous, glad
    That his friend of a lifetime was there,
Though it's true it was late on a *really* bad date
    In the lives of the Ludicrous pair.

"Over here, by the wall at the end of the hall,"
    Came instructions from out of the dark,
And Pragmaticus crept like a canny adept
    Till the end of his nose hit the mark.

NEBULOUS IN LOVE

But before he could bend to console his best friend
    On the unpleasant business ahead,
His old chum spoke up first in a blubbering burst
    And begged *him* for forgiveness instead:

"Oh, Pragmaticus, friend, may the heavens forfend!
    You shall never again be abused
By the friend who would force you to marry that *horse*
    By his failure, which can't be excused;

"For in friendship you came – not a friend just in name,
    But a friend who was willing and fit –
But in spite of your help you'll wed Sleazum's young whelp,
    And your future's as bleak as the pit.

"So forgive me, I pray, on my last mortal day,
    Before dawn finds me dead in this brig;
It was my lot to fail in this Earthly travail;
    It is yours that you marry that pig."

As Pragmaticus sat to continue their chat
    He forgave his old pal for his fate,
For he already knew Hunkus hadn't come through
    In the little dark room by the gate.

LeRoy Carl Blake

"Oh, it counts not at all that you fumbled the ball
    Like the affable klutz you can be,
And that Flatula swore that the Hunk didn't score,
    Which of course leaves her free to wed me,

"But I think it's a shame how my sister can claim
    Still to be so enamored of *you;*
She came crying to me to make Dad set you free,
    Even after what you tried to do.

"Yet, she swore by the grace of Minerva's fair face
    That she kisses the hem of your cloak,
And she gave me your clothes to return, I suppose,
    So you'll have something on when you croak.

"And it's only because you get all her applause
    That I stole here before morning light;
For she swore loud and long that the Hunk was all wrong
    When he said that you raped her tonight."

"And *I* swear that is so! Surely both of you know,"
    Bellowed Nebulous, angry by then,
"I was saving her life, and I'd face any strife
    To be near her to save her again."

NEBULOUS IN LOVE

"It is not her 'again' that needs help, gentlemen,"
    Said Pragmaticus. "May I remind?
She is safe in the care of my mother somewhere,
    While *you* are, in a word, in a bind."

"With all deference, lad, is our plight all that bad?"
    They heard Virtuous quietly ask,
"And why shut up my son in this palace of fun
    When the Carcer was built for that task?"

As a blueblood is taught, young Pragmaticus thought:
    I'll not add to the old man's regrets;
Thus, to soften the blow of his tidings of woe
    He said, "Man, it's as bad as it gets!

"And the reason you're here in this chapel of cheer
    Is to keep all the riffraff away,
So my dad can move fast when the sun's up at last,
    Without having some hick cause delay.

"And his logic is sound, you'll agree all around,
    For the crowd rather likes you, I fear,
But at first light of day they'll be kept well away
    At the Carcer 'til Pater's done here."

LeROY CARL BLAKE

Now then, Nebulous smiled at the cunning, if wild,
    Way Pragmaticus' dad wielded power:
To deny him support at the kangaroo court
    That would lop off his head in an hour.

He was all set to say it was his lucky day
    To be there when the court would convene,
When from outside the door came a gawd-awful roar
    And three figures burst in on the scene.

Of the trio that bore through the flung-open door,
    Two Imperial Guards stood out tall;
But the one in the middle presented a riddle,
    For no one could see him at all.

Quickly, Nebulous rose in a body with those who were crouched
    'Neath the dark, smoky veil,
As he struggled to see who the poor fool could be
    Who would share in his tavern-cum-jail.

But the furious rage of a bear in a cage
    (Well, to Virtuous and to the boys)
Seemed as tame in its way as a kitten at play
    When compared to this new, evil noise

NEBULOUS IN LOVE

Of the middle man's shouts as he screeched at the louts
    Where to go and how long they should stay,
And they answered in turn with true Guardsmen's concern:
    "Ah, shut up or you'll blow your toupee!"

The Guards, having thus spake, slammed the door in their wake
    After dumping their charge on the floor
Where he cursed a blue streak, venting most of his cheek
    On his dearly belov'd Emperor:

"Oh, you dumber than dumb! You drunk, sweaty-faced bum!
    How could anyone, dumb as you are,
Take the side of that ass from the crude, merchant class,
    Against *me* – wondrous Rome's brightest star!

"Do you hear? You're a *bum!* You unwashed, drunken scum,
    And by Heaven, when I'm out of here,
The great year Sixty-Nine will forever enshrine
    In its total your lousy career!"

Such a visceral threat (From a prisoner, yet!)
    Against Feckless' perpetual spree
Left the others in shock as they slowly took stock
    Of just who their new roommate must be.

LeROY CARL BLAKE

For, abuse to the crown, so divinely low-down,
    So deliciously loud and pugnacious,
Could have only been wrung from the sweet silver tongue
    Of none other than . . . Grievous Vexatious!

"You have got to be joking!" Pragmaticus, choking,
    Tried bravely, if weakly, to stammer;
"You're the last man, I'd think, who'd get stuck in the stink
    Of this smoke-sullied, substitute slammer."

"What! Is that my dear boy?" cried Vexatious with joy
    And a laugh, underscoring the point;
Then his voice became stern with paternal concern,
    And he said, "Why are *you* in the Joint?"

"I have promised my friend to keep watch till the end,"
    The boy said in a voice firm and clear,
"But the moment draws nigh when my best friend will die,
    Thanks to Hunkus and you, Father dear."

Then Vexatious saw red: his blood boiled as he said,
    "I'm as stripped as a sheep that's been shorn!
First, I'm cast in this pit by that drunk, witless twit;
    Then Pragmaticus shows me *his* scorn!

NEBULOUS IN LOVE

"Oh, great gods! *Are you there?* Are you deaf to my prayer
      To rain blessings on my noble house?
You keep raining, instead, stupid woes on my head,
      Like this son who would comfort that *louse!*

"You have tweaked my old nose and beset me with foes
      Who deny me my moment of glory,
When in truth all I seek is the head of this geek,
      And a warm, loving end to my story."

Then the Senator fell to his knees in the cell
      Which was really Juturna's cold inn,
And his wail filled the air at how cruelly unfair
      All the gods in Rome's Heaven had been.

"Gee, I hate to intrude on so sacred a mood,"
      Whispered Nebulous when it was done,
"But I think you should know that it just isn't so
      About my having raped anyone."

"Why, you asinine *goof!* I have absolute proof!
      Wasn't Hunkus, the officer, there?
And, if I'm not too rude, weren't you caught in the nude
      With your tush coolly fanning the air?

LeRoy Carl Blake

"Do you think me a fool, or a boy out of school,
      Or an oaf who's not keenly aware
Since the moment you met you've been trying to get
      Into my little girl's underwear?

"You were warned twice before not to darken her door,
      But you chose to ignore my fair warning;
Well, I let you escape from our first little scrape,
      But you'll not be so lucky this morning!

"Just because I'm in here gives you no cause for cheer;
      I can still have your head in a flash!
All the Guard has to know is that I want it so
      (Plus, of course, a small payment in cash);

"So if you have a prayer for the goddess 'up there'
      Who loves poets and sayers of sooth,
Then get down on your knees while I call the bribees
      And prepare for your moment of truth."

Slowly, Nebulous turned to the one most concerned
      With his fate on that black, hopeless day,
And he kissed his old dad for what might have been, had
      He not willfully gone so astray.

NEBULOUS IN LOVE

And, as sadly he knelt, the contrition he felt
    Wasn't dimmed when Vexatious brought in
A Praetorian slob who would finish the job
    His arrest was designed to begin.

But, when down on his knees with his neck stretched to please,
    He thought, *This is foolhardiness' price,*
For life could have been grand and gone just as Dad planned
    If I'd taken my best friend's advice;

For Pragmaticus said: "Straighten out or you're dead,"
    But I stubbornly stayed on my cloud,
Just like Phallus, the twit! Then it suddenly hit:
    "Where *is* Phallus?" he blurted out loud.

"What is Phallus to you," roared the Senator, who
    Was impatient with any delay.
"You're distracting the lad with the sword, and that's bad.
    Settle down or we'll be here all day."

"But I think you should know before I, er, well, *go,*
    That you're helping him make his escape;
While you're fooling with me he is footloose and free,
    And he's getting away with near rape."

"You're the rapist I see, so don't pull that on me!
      Do you think you'll escape judgment day?
And besides, when I'm through with what I'm going to do,
      You won't care about him anyway."

Then Pragmaticus said, "Before cleaving his head,
      I attest that his story is true:
The old Celt was to blame for poor Nebulous' shame,
      And he ventured to rape Ampla, too."

"Are you trying to say *both* men wanted their way
      With my budding young pearl of the vine,
But the Celt skipped away in the froth of the fray
      When the Hunk saved her honor – and mine?

"Then I swear to you, Son, when our work here is done
      We'll track down that depraved escapee!
Before this day is through we'll have had his head, too,
      For his arrogant insult to *me!*"

"There's a misapprehension that's causing the tension,"
      Said Nebulous, "and I confess
It was Phallus' fat gumption and Hunkus' presumption
      That got us all into this mess.

NEBULOUS IN LOVE

"And we've gone far enough with this head chopping stuff,
    Because Phallus, not me, is the man
Who sought Ampla's sweet trust in his boudoir of lust,
    Leaving me to get caught when he ran."

Now the Guard was perplexed, with his muscles all flexed
    To deliver a swift, downward blow,
And he told the small crowd, "Oh, for crying out loud,
    Hold him still or I'll pack up and go!"

Disregarding the Guard, the old Solon yelled, "Bard,
    You're the one that I have here with me,
And I'm not unaware you were captured down *there*,
    Which means you are as guilty as he."

"Ampla asked me to say it just wasn't that way,"
    Sighed Pragmaticus. "Under duress,
The Celt lured her downstairs where – so help me, she swears –
    She was duped into doffing her dress.

"But when Nebulous showed, the old Celt hit the road
    Through a hole in the wall, by the bed;
By the time Hunk was there he'd gone up in thin air,
    So Hunk 'captured' my pal here instead."

LeROY CARL BLAKE

Now the Guardsman was mad, for the neck of the lad,
    First appraised with a confident smile,
Kept on dodging around way too high off the ground,
    And his swing missed the mark by a mile.

"Since you're so bloody smart, then begin at the start,"
    Yelled Vexatious, and grabbed for the hair
Of young Nebulous, who he jerked nearly in two
    As a second swing sliced through the air.

"And don't fill me with stories of gods in their glories
    Or love potions plucked from a tree,"
The old Senator spat. Then he knocked the boy flat
    As the air hissed with swing number three.

Quickly, Nebulous told how a friendship of gold
    Turned to hatred beclouded by lust,
Because Phallus felt used when Vexatious refused
    To betroth him his daughter in trust;

How he'd heard Phallus vow – well, he swore, anyhow –
    That he'd mount Ample's fair maidenhood
Like a souvenir pelt, or a notch on his belt,
    Just as soon as he possibly could;

NEBULOUS IN LOVE

And that, last but not least, Phallus' elegant feast
    Held to honor the groom and the bride
Was no more than a plot by the fat, rather squat,
    Old poseur to avenge wounded pride.

"It now seems rather clear, since we're both stuck in here,"
    Went on Nebulous, "Phallus, before
He slipped out through his gate, sealed our mutual fate."
    As he rose he dodged swing number four.

Then, when Nebulous stopped, hatred suddenly dropped
    From the look in Vexatious' cold eyes,
And the man who'd behead the young poet, instead
    Stretched his hand out and helped him to rise.

"It becomes plain as day, with us both shut away,"
    Said Vexatious, now thoroughly vexed,
"That he'd have the last laugh reading your epitaph,
    Knowing mine was the one he'd read next."

"Well, I've thought about that, and I think we should chat,"
    The old Solon heard Nebulous say,
"Because while it is true that I'm stuck here with you,
    There's no reason for staying that way.

"If we both can't be free, then it seems fair to me
        That if *one* can escape he should fly,
For to leave Phallus loose would be pulling a noose
        Around both of our necks till we die.

"So, I hereby propose, by the hues of my nose,
        That you hasten me well on my way,
Because you need the clout of that drunk to get out,
        Whereas I simply need *your* OK."

But Vexatious got mad and again shoved the lad,
        Who lurched backward and tried not to fall,
As the frustrated Guard swung so shockingly hard,
        When he missed he went down in a sprawl.

"Do not think you can flee just like that and leave *me*,"
        Roared Vexatious, "while you and the Gaul
And, as likely as not, the Imperial Sot,
        Plot together to hasten my fall!

"With me out of the way it will be a field day
        Between Phallus, His Highness, and you –
You could marry my girl in a wink and a twirl
        While *they* split my estate 'twixt the two."

NEBULOUS IN LOVE

And as Grievous bored in, standing there, shin to shin
    With the object of making his point,
The Guard spat out some teeth, rammed his sword in its sheath,
    And observed as he limped from the joint,

"That's the trouble today with these kids and the way
    They're allowed to grow up with no pride!
If this brat had been mine he'd have shown 'em more spine:
    He'd have stayed put and properly *died!*"

"But you don't understand!" The boy put up his hand
    To keep seething Vexatious at bay
While he tried to explain – he presumed not in vain –
    Why he needed to leave right away:

"While we're held under lock in this make-believe dock,
    All the ills of the world can beset us;
But indulge me this boon and we'll both be free soon,
    Ere the Guards walk away and forget us.

"For, the problems for you – I'm afraid there are two –
    Are that Sleazum is after your son,
While of course the old Celt, with an eye for the svelte,
    Wants your daughter for his Number One.

LeRoy Carl Blake

"So, there's no room for doubt when you sort it all out:
        It's the Sleaze that presents the real threat,
For while you are in here and he's out, free and clear,
        You'll need all of the help you can get.

"Now – don't hit me again I know just where both men
        Can be found, and what I have to do
To get Sleaze off your case, put the Celt in his place,
        Help my father, and come rescue you."

"Why should I believe that?" snapped Vexatious, and sat
        By the others, up next to the wall.
"For if I set you free, you will run out on me
        And join Feckless, the Sleaze, and the Gaul!"

"Hold your chatter, you two, or you'll never break through
        Your pathetic impasse of suspicion,"
Came a voice which they'd heard utter nary a word
        Since Vexatious was given admission.

"For your plan to succeed, what you both really need,"
        The proud father of Nebulous said,
"Is a hostage to stay with Vexatious today
        As a surrogate chopable head,

NEBULOUS IN LOVE

So Vexatious can know, and quite rightfully so,
      He has someone on hand he can kill;
I do therefore propose, when young Nebulous goes,
      I be given that task to fulfill."

"Oh, no!" Nebulous cried, "I'd be lost if you died
      Because I, through pure chance (Or pure greed?)
Failed to carry the day or, you know, ran away,
      Leaving you to remain here and bleed."

"But I love it! It's done!" yelled Vexatious. "The son
      Will be sure to help Daddy survive
By discharging his vow to bail *me* out somehow,
      And bring Sleaze and the Celt here alive."

So, the Number One man among Senators ran
      To prepare the men guarding the door
To let Nebulous go on his way, even though
      He still sported his head, as before.

"Um, there *is* one thing more which we shouldn't ignore,"
      Put in Nebulous. "While you hold Pater,
I insist you accept, if our bargain be kept,
      A condition which I shall name later."

LeROY CARL BLAKE

"Who are you to *insist?* What you'll get is my fist
      If you don't haul your butt from this place!"
Screeched the bellicose bore, in a temper once more,
      Breathing fire into Nebulous' face.

"We have just made a deal in which I will repeal
      All my charges and just let you go
In return for which you will then rescue me, too,
      Which is known as a straight *quid pro quo*."

"And you'd like that, because I'd be back where I *was*,"
      Hollered Nebulous, standing his ground.
"Well, my lord, it's a cinch I'm not moving an inch
      Till you swear that my wish holds you bound."

Now they stood toe to toe in the smoldering glow,
      Neither man giving way to the other,
Till Pragmaticus spoke to his dad through the smoke
      As one speaks to an errant kid brother:

"Look, it's not going to fly until you say good-bye
      To your pain-in-the-ass attitude,
For with both of you here *You are dead, do you hear?*
      So come off it and quit being rude."

NEBULOUS IN LOVE

The old man fairly shook as he fastened his look
>   On the son who had dared speak the truth,
Who, for all of his zits had a head full of wits
>   In an otherwise average youth:

"I agree, if I must, to all terms that are just,
>   And accept your unstated condition,"
Growled Vexatious at length, "And I yield on the strength
>   Of your rank as a Roman Patrician."

"Let's get out of here then!" Whooped Pragmaticus, when
>   He saw Nebulous free to depart;
"You should be on your way and stop wasting the day,
>   And I'm coming along, so let's *start*."

So, with soot on their faces and farewell embraces,
>   They bade both their fathers good-bye,
Then they opened the door on the Guards' merry snore
>   And the first rosy rays in the sky.

"Look, I haven't a clue as to how you will do
>   All you plan to get done on this day,"
Young Pragmaticus laughed, "And you must think me daft
>   For my offer to help in some way,

"But if you'll be so kind, please just keep it in mind
    That my purpose in taking this chance
Is that Flatula dear draws disgustingly near
    And I'm hoping we'll stop her advance."

"All good things in due time," answered Nebulous. "I'm
    Listing Flatula as an addendum,
But what's first on the list is a good-morning tryst
    With the infamous Renta Pudendum."

And, as Nebulous talked, the boys rapidly walked
    Up the steps to the very top street
To a door that was locked, on which Nebulous knocked,
    'Neath a sign which read "Renta's Retreat."

CHAPTER FOURTEEN

"Why on Earth are we *here?*" asked Pragmaticus. "We're
    Surely not wasting time on *these* dames?
Our great mission today isn't yet under way,
    So don't tell me you want to play games!"

"No, the reason we're here should be perfectly clear,"
    Whispered Nebulous. "Can't you but guess?"
Where would you have retired if each hour you required
    A new batch of young things to caress?"

The door parted a crack and a pretty young black,
    Squinting hard in the light, softly swore:
"Look, we all stayed up late, so unless you can't *wait*,
    I suggest you come back around four."

"Thank you, ma'am, but we've come not to lie with your scum,"
    Replied Nebulous, beaming a smile,
"But to tell the Praefectus – that's Phallus Erectus –
    We'll go with him now to his trial.

LeRoy Carl Blake

"And it must be made clear, if you hide him in here,
    In this sweet-scented, soft citadel,
You must never forget that to aid and abet
    A known felon makes you one as well."

Though the Nubian face never moved from its place,
    The boys' message was quick to get through:
The big door opened wide, and there, sitting inside,
    Was the Celt and an all-girl revue.

"And to what, if I may, do I owe this display
    Of bright noses and false accusations?"
Asked the Celt with a grin as he lost himself in
    The delights of the girls' ministrations.

"Oh, the charge against *you* is inflexibly true,"
    Said Pragmaticus. "Here are the facts:
My dear Father just said: 'I will cut off his head!'
    When he learned of your devious acts."

Now the Celt swallowed hard and sweat oozed from the lard
    As he tried to sort out what to do,
For he knew he was trapped, though protectively wrapped
    In a dozen bare bodies or two.

NEBULOUS IN LOVE

"Such exceptional boys need exceptional toys,"
    Phallus finally said with a smile;
"May I offer to pay for a spring holiday
    While you vanish in Spain for a while?"

"I've an offer for you, if you're sure you are through
    With such pettiness," Nebulous said.
"I am in a position, for one small condition,
    To guarantee saving your head."

"Why would you guarantee to save someone like me?"
    Prompted Phallus, abruptly on guard;
"And 'conditions,' as such, don't appeal to me much
    When proposed by a starveling bard."

"I will let you go free to be useful to me,"
    Replied Nebulous, blunting his voice.
"And you'll meet my condition in humble submission,
    Because, sir, you've no other choice."

"And just what must I do to accommodate you?"
    Phallus haughtily started to scoff;
Then he quickly broke out in a little-boy pout
    When the girls all got up and walked off.

"Well! Do you believe that? *They just left me here flat!*
 Or, just maybe this isn't my day."
But he quickly revived when the day shift arrived
 Freshly scented and eager to play.

"I will name my condition without inhibition,"
 Said Nebulous, closing debate,
"At the stroke of high noon by Juturna's lagoon –
 If you value your life, don't be late!"

As they turned from the scene of the man in between
 All the shimmering arms, legs, and curls,
Only Nebulous knew it would take a whole crew
 To get Phallus away from his girls.

"We're in trouble again," whispered Nebulous then.
 "Oh, Pragmaticus, I don't see how
We can get him to jail so my scheme can prevail,
 Since we *must* visit Spectra right now."

"Are you shaking my tree?" laughed Pragmaticus. "Gee,
 I can have him there *yesterday* noon.
But I sort of was hoping that we could start coping
 With *my* little problem – and soon?"

NEBULOUS IN LOVE

"Not to worry, my friend, you'll be saved in the end,"
      Promised Nebulous, "later today.
First, the trap must be set if we're ever to get
      Fetid Flatula out of the way."

"All my faith is in you," choked Pragmaticus, who,
      Feeling hope bursting through in his joy,
Gripped his friend by the hand and cried, "Go where you planned!
      I will stay and take care of our boy."

They shook hands at the door and young Nebulous swore
      He had faith that his pal would come through;
Then he stepped to the street in the day's rising heat
      And made straight for his great rendezvous.

He checked out every home on the best street in Rome
      To find Spectra's abode there among,
But when Nebulous neared all his pluck disappeared
      On recalling the widow's sharp tongue.

So he stood in his good mint-condition manhood
      Psyching up for the grand confrontation
While remaining perplexed as to what to do next,
      And he felt like a kid on probation.

LeRoy Carl Blake

When he finally knocked and the door was unlocked,
        He was asked if he'd please step inside
To the welcoming shade by a lovely young maid,
        Where he nearly jumped out of his hide.

Alas, who should be there with her come-hither stare
        And her tongue through her teeth like a dart,
But Coita-The-Pure, who, in crimson velour,
        Showed the tiniest trace of a tart.

"Well, good morning to *you*," she proceeded to coo,
        "And to what do I owe this surprise?
Are you ready to play with the big girls today,
        Or to just – if you must – fantasize?"

"You stay out of my way!" the lad managed to say,
        Feeling suddenly twenty times worse.
"Please announce that I'm here and then just *disappear*
        So that Spectra and I may converse."

"Why are you so uptight (Are you sure you're all right)?"
        Asked Coita, her hand on his thigh;
"All I wanted to do was to get to know you,
        But you don't want to give it a try.

NEBULOUS IN LOVE

"Say, I have an idea! A first-rate panacea
    For losing your cool around me:
Let us go and lie down; you can drop off my gown,
    And I'll drop my tutorial fee."

Now her hand was inside of his robe, where she tried
    To find out why he stood on his toes;
He kept backing away, so her hand couldn't stay.
    As her hand fell, our Nebulous rose.

"I do hate to intrude, but you're both being lewd,"
    Said a voice from the far peristyle.
"Let him go now, you tramp, then make tracks and decamp.
    I will speak with this crass juvenile."

With a lingering pout Fair Coita strode out,
    Leaving Nebulous weak in the knees,
And as Spectra approached he was sure he'd encroached
    On her morning of insular ease.

"Um, good morrow, Madame. Er, that is, here I am.
    I mean, finding you here is so pleasant."
Why did he always feel like a teenage schlemiel
    Every time that this woman was present?

LeRoy Carl Blake

"Oh, I'm sure it feels grand finding Spectra on hand
      To protect you from Coita's gropes,"
Said the matronly frau with the simian brow,
      "And to peel your behind off the ropes,

"But from where I am sitting it's pointedly fitting
      To say you aren't wroth with my sister,
Unless you've grown a sword or a calabash gourd,
      Or you're raising a world record blister?

"But enough of this chat. It is clear to me that
      You've not come to engage in more quibbling,
But to tell me, instead, whom Coita will wed,
      Freeing me from that brat of a sibling.

"Well, you've come a bit late to name Coita's mate,
      For the bargain between us is dead.
I am not going to bother to marry your father,
      In spite of the low overhead.

"True, I'll miss the acclaim of the Ludicrous name,
      But a union would now be unsound,
Because after last night there's a terrible blight
      On that name which was once so renowned.

NEBULOUS IN LOVE

"And don't think just because I provided no clause
      In my deal to betroth your old man
Which expressly forbids that he have crazy kids,
      That I have to go through with the plan.

"No, the man whom I said I would happily wed
      Had a name that was wholesome and pure,
But your fool's escapade has turned that accolade
      To industrial strength horse manure.

"So the answer is 'no,' and with that you may go.
      I don't care to what you may aspire.
Your behavior last night put the last dream to flight
      Of my cohabitative desire."

"My dear lady! Last night was no grand plebiscite –
      I was bagged at the whim of one guy!
And by dawn even he had to let me go free,
      Because he knew the charge was a lie.

"Now I ask, do I look like the kind of a schnook
      Who would cheat about losing his head?
If I were, you could tell by a rather quaint smell:
      I'd be walking around slightly dead.

"But the point is, I'm free because Phallus, not me
        Is the one who attempted the rape,
And my father's good name – may it bring him acclaim! –
        Is in truly formidable shape.

"So throw open your heart to a bold, brand new start
        As the wife of a noble Patrician,
And Coita will stand at the altar as planned
        With the Hunk of ignoble ambition."

Now a silence was all that was heard in the hall,
        and poor Nebulous' heart filled with dread
That the lady, somehow, might refuse even now.
        But she didn't. She quietly said:

"From the hue of your nose – like a blossoming rose –
        You have paid for another man's crime;
I am filled with remorse that I judged you, of course,
        Though you *looked* like a schnook at the time.

"And I also am filled with a joy undistilled
        That it's Hunkus my sister will wed;
Though he's sort of an ass, his *behind* is world class
        And he'll keep her, I hope, in one bed.

NEBULOUS IN LOVE

"And now what may I do to accommodate you
    In repayment for all you've endured?
(As a word to the wise, I would strongly advise
    That these weddings be quickly secured.)"

"That, dear madam, of course is the reason, perforce,
    That I came to your door at this hour;
For your husbands await – in their ignorant state –
    For your hearts, and your hands, and your dower.

"Fetch your sister, I pray and we'll make straightaway
    For the Forum and destiny's call,
That is, if 'The Behind' i.e. Hunkus defined,
    Can be tricked into taking the fall."

Now the sun was half way from pink dawn to midday,
    Which made Nebulous keenly aware
Of the time as it flew and what he had to do
    To make use of this sisterly pair:

First, he *must* tell his dad, who would feel he'd been had,
    Then find Hunk and Emporium, too;
But regardless of that his whole plan would fall flat
    If Pragmaticus failed to come through.

LeRoy Carl Blake

All this weight on his mind, plus the sisters, combined
    With the fact that he'd left his old man
With Vexatious to die if he didn't comply
    Made him doubt, for the first time, his plan.

Could it be that he'd fail? Or would true love prevail?
    Would the Fates of his dad interfere?
He could barely think straight in his feverish state,
    And his options were not at all clear.

So, when Spectra – discreet, dressed in clothes for the street –
    Reappeared with Coita in tow,
Lowly Nebulous said: "Though they all think we're dead,
    We will show them who's who! Now let's Go!"

CHAPTER FIFTEEN

On a normal spring day all the great rights-of-way
    Leading into the Forum were rife
With the hordes in pursuit of their daily commute
    Toward the fulcrum of civilized life.

But on this azure day in what's called the New Way,
    On the flank of the Palatine hill,
Two Patricians walked proud through the midst of that crowd
    As it ground through the great Roman mill.

"I *do* hope you've the sense not to make a defense
    For the way that fool acted last night,"
Said the one with white hair to his obvious heir
    As they came to the stair and turned right.

"For if you were to try to stand up for the guy
    For the sake of the deal that you made,
And if *then* Feckless said to whack off his fat head,
    You can guess who'd be next on the blade!"

LeRoy Carl Blake

"Ah, but Sire, you'll agree, in our whole family
    It's the best deal that's ever been won:
He'll endorse my demand for a gen'ral's command,
    And keep at it until it's been done."

"*If* he makes it, indeed! When will you ever heed
    That discretion is nine tenths of valor,
And a fool and his head end up separately dead,
    With an irreconcilable pallor!

"Hunk, I'm counting on you and you'd better come through!"
    Gorgeosus was arguing fast.
"Things have changed since last night when I made you do right
    And give in to Vexatious' bombast.

"As you saw very well, the man blew it to hell
    When he ticked off Despoticus first,
Then he got in it deep when he savaged that creep,
    And he wound up completely *immersed*.

"And believe me, it's true! It will rub off on *you*
    If you don't begin using your head;
There is no doubt about it, you'll wind up without it;
    In fact, you'll have *both of us* dead."

NEBULOUS IN LOVE

So, with no false illusion that Hunkus' delusion
    Of saving Vexatious would wane,
Gorgeosus adhered to the scion he'd reared
    To make sure he did nothing insane.

Thus it was he contrived, as they quickly arrived
    At the inn at the foot of the stair,
That both father and son would now see things as one
    In their view of this messy affair.

But his countenance fell – and his prospects, as well –
    As he glanced at the Forum beyond,
Where he spotted the Sleaze who was batting the breeze
    At a run toward Juturna's old pond.

"What are *you* doing here? *How dare you interfere!*"
    Panted Sleazum while gasping for air;
"If you'd speak with Vexatious you're just too audacious
    For even Minerva to bear!

"For Vexatious, in fact, due to foul lack of tact,
    Still awaits the Imperial Court,
And he'll get what he's due despite toadies like you
    With your fawning, pathetic support."

LeRoy Carl Blake

"But, good Sleazum, please know I'm accustomed to go
    To the temple each day by this route.
Why link *me* with last night and your pitiful fight?"
    Gorgeosus asked, looking devout.

"You don't scare me a bit with your classy-ass wit,"
    Scoffed the wine merchant, curling his lip.
"You need Ampla's old dad, and you need him real bad,
    'Cause without him Hunk's wedding is zip.

"But I'll give you this news: Glib Vexatious can choose
    From three options he holds as of now.
First, I'll drop my denouncement upon this announcement:
    His son gives my daughter his vow.

"Or, the next choice – but worse – I'll throw chapter and verse
    Of the battery law in his face
If he thinks he can win litigation wherein
    Half of Rome saw his utter disgrace;

"And the third choice is this: should my plan go amiss
    And he's able to salvage his life,
I'll make very well known to the man on the throne
    That Vexatious once diddled his wife!"

NEBULOUS IN LOVE

Hunkus looked at his dad, and things looked pretty bad
    From the depth of the older man's frown,
But a glance up the stair took him quite unaware
    When he saw who it was coming down.

"Pater, how can this be? I mean, gads! Isn't he
    The dumb bard that I gave to Vexatious?
Well, your gripping insistence to crush my resistance
    Turned out to be pretty fallacious."

Even Sleaze dropped his jaw as the three stood in awe
    Of the trio so far up the stair,
For there wasn't a doubt, from his blossoming snout
    Whom they saw with two women up there.

Gorgeosus was first, being clearly well versed
    In the business of using his head,
Of the three surprised gents to recover his sense
    And he blurted, "It can't be! He's dead!"

"Well he's sure as hell *back*," growled the huckstering hack,
    "From wherever in Hades he went,
And if he went to Hades it means that those ladies
    Are not what you'd call Heaven-sent."

LeRoy Carl Blake

So they waited below, each man eager to know
    What the coming of Nebulous meant,
While the lad, in his turn, watched with anxious concern
    As he wound through the crowd in descent.

But as Nebulous' eyes caught the look of surprise
    On the Welcome Committee of three,
He was also aware of the absence down there
    Of the one he most wanted to see:

"Oh, Pragmaticus, man, since this caper began,"
    Whispered Nebulous, knitting his brow,
"I have not needed you half as much as I do
    At this minute, so don't fail me now!"

With his countenance set (And his palms wet with sweat)
    And Coita pressed close at his side,
Bravely Nebulous stepped down the stairs and was swept
    Toward his fate on the Forum-bound tide.

Gorgeosus, no fool, showed his usual cool
    As he quickly took over command
Of his truculent troop on the inn's stony stoop,
    And stepped forward to put out his hand.

NEBULOUS IN LOVE

"Hail and welcome to you and your lady friends too,
    Noble Nebulous, bruised but unbowed!
Though your nose looks surreal, you survived your ordeal."
    You'd look better to me in a shroud!

"Thank you, Senator, sir. May I say I concur,"
    Countered Nebulous. Hunkus just glared.
"And you're looking well, too." *Which is probably due*
    To some poisonous plot you've prepared.

"Now, what news of the day got you up and away,
    And now keeps you from home and your bed?"
Gorgeosus then asked while he kept his thoughts masked.
    "Why, I'd think that by now you'd be dead."

"Oh, I'm weary, all right. Yes, it *was* a long night,
    But the reason I've come to this inn
Is to look for dear Pater, your fellow debater,
    Who sits with Vexatious, within."

"Well, you'll see your dad soon, for it's already noon,"
    Snickered Sleaze, "when the life-or-death fate
Of Vexatious will be, by and large, up to me
    Which is why, you schlemiel, I can't wait!"

LeRoy Carl Blake

But, as Sleazum rejoiced, a young Guards captain voiced
    To the group by the door on the stoop,
That, by Hades, he vowed he had raced through the crowd
    From the Palace to bring them this scoop:

"For all who await the Great God of our State,
    Be it known that His Highness will not
Grace the Forum this day – at least not right away –
    Largely due to the headache he's got.

"What is more, from his bed he reportedly said
    That remembrance, as usual, is gone;
He can't even recall how he got home at all,
    Let alone what he did until dawn.

"So if you want to wait, the Divine Reprobate
    Should be up and about around three,
Though the guys in the know say he's not gonna show –
    But don't say that you heard it from me."

"You. . .*you're making that up!* You young mange-covered pup."
    Bellowed Sleazum, now fearing the suit
He had brought in the name of his ticket to fame
    Was in danger of getting the boot.

NEBULOUS IN LOVE

"Honored Sleazum, do please set your worries at ease,"
    Offered Nebulous, trying his best,
"For there's naught we can do to make dead dreams come true,
    So in Heaven's name give it a rest!

"Furthermore, I implore you to quickly explore
    Compromises whereby you'll save face,
For as you can now see, if Vexatious goes free
    He will see to your total disgrace."

"*Not in ten thousand years!*" screamed the merchant, in tears
    At the infamous turn of events.
"Do you think I'm so dumb that I'll quit when I've come
    To the goal of my baser intents?

"If that ward-heeling hack can't recall the attack
    For which *he* said the man must atone,
I'll stick this in his head: it's Lascivia's bed
    That Vexatious prefers to his own!

"Then let's see what that clown with the twigs-and-leaves crown
    Wants his buddy, Vexatious, to do:
Will he let him go free? Or would you all agree
    That by nightfall he'll chop him in two!"

LeRoy Carl Blake

"Sleazum," Nebulous said, "you're not using your head!
      For while vengeance is sweet, it is true,
You have nothing to gain if Vexatious is slain,
      For then Flatula's future dies, too.

"Since the god didn't show, it means he's free to go –
      Any minute they'll bring him outside –
If you'll just compromise, you may salvage the prize
      Of the status you seek *and* your pride."

Seeing no other choice, the Guards captain gave voice
      To commands to the men at their posts
To bring forth from the gloom of the smoky old room
      A matched pair of old, soot-covered ghosts.

As Vexatious stepped out, groping blindly about
      In the glare from the brassy blue skies,
He tried bravely to hide all the terror inside
      While he squinted with light-blinded eyes.

Then came Nebulous' dad, who observably had
      Struggled bravely to keep his belief,
Who then rushed to the side of the source of his pride
      And embraced him with untold relief:

NEBULOUS IN LOVE

"Oh, I *knew* you'd arrive to find me still alive
      By midday! But as seventh hour beckoned
I was in a right state – how could I know you'd wait
      To show up till the very last second?"

At the sight of the man by whom Nebulous' plan
      Gave her blue-blooded status this day,
Hideosa drew nigh and with joy heaved a sigh
      As the pain in her heart fell away.

And the look of surprise that lit Virtuous' eyes
      When he witnessed her beautiful smile
Let him see that her love was a gift from above
      (Not to mention her wit and her style).

But Vexatious knew well he had heard his death knell
      When they led him from where he was jailed:
They would spill his blue blood – on the spot, in the mud! –
      Meaning Nebulous surely had failed.

But his sight soon returned and, although his eyes burned,
      To Vexatious the truth became clear:
The Imperial sot was nowhere on the lot,
      And not likely, it seemed, to appear.

LeRoy Carl Blake

What he did see, instead, as his dread quickly fled,
    Was that Sleazum stood there looking back:
Like a togated streak with a blood-chilling shriek,
    He leaped over the guards to attack.

As he clutched at the throat of the grasping old goat
    He felt murderous joy in his heart;
It took all of the strength of the others, at length,
    To pry Sleaze and Vexatious apart.

"By the gods, keep it cool and quit playing the fool!"
    Whispered Nebulous into his ear.
"If you want to get sprung you *need* Sleazum's glib tongue,
    So quit trying to kill him, you hear?"

With his pride knocked askew, Grievous strained as he drew
    On some great, inner strength to relax,
Though he glowed with the fire of his burning desire
    To part Sleazum's thin hair with an axe.

When at last he was quiet and fears of a riot
    Were down an iota or two,
Quickly, Nebulous spoke – bravely going for broke –
    And Vexatious was told what to do.

NEBULOUS IN LOVE

"You'd tell *me* to behave? You obstreperous knave!"
  The old Senator bellowed right back.
"I'm a man of reserve made of ironclad nerve,
  And what's more, I can fake what I lack!"

"I am telling you, sire, that the fat's in the fire,"
  Whispered Nebulous, all his fear gone.
"Now I want your submission to my bold condition
  As promised this morning at dawn."

"What's that promise to me now that I'll be set free?"
  Laughed Vexatious in Nebulous' face.
"Surely you don't believe I'll be given to grieve
  For a promise I break in *your* case?"

"What I cannot believe is that you're so naïve,"
  Answered Nebulous, weary of trying,
"That you just will not see that between Sleaze and me
  Lies your choice between living and dying.

"And your only escape from the hands of that ape
  Is to give me your unalloyed trust,
And to honor your pledge without hassle or hedge
  To accept my condition as just."

LeRoy Carl Blake

Now Vexatious, in truth, really *hated* this youth
    With his rainbow-hued nose out of joint,
But way down deep inside, beyond reach of his pride,
    He knew Nebulous made a good point.

"Oh, don't get so upset, you teen-age martinet!
    You've my word as a noble patrician:
I do now set my seal to your 'qualified deal.'
    Now, just *what is* your stupid 'condition?'"

"Thank the gods you concur in our enterprise, sir!
    My condition is fair as can be:
Forgive Phallus, that's all – after all, he's a Gaul –
    Then give Ampla in marriage to me."

"Why, you ding-a-ling ditz with your face full of zits!
    The Celt wanted to diddle my girl!
Do you really believe I won't happily cleave
    His fat head from the rest of that churl?

"And how dare you demand my sweet Ampla's fair hand
    In the same breath you bid me forgive
What that cretin has done in his warped sense of fun,
    Which I swear he will never outlive!

NEBULOUS IN LOVE

"It was *you* convinced *me*, you contemptible flea,
    That the Celt is the culprit to blame;
Let me stand face to face with that Gallic disgrace
    And I'll rub his fat nose in his shame!"

But that, Nebulous knew, he could not quickly do
    If Pragmaticus didn't come soon
With the Celt that he swore would be here at the door
    Of Juturna's old hostel by noon.

Now, though Grievous' felt burned, all the others had turned
    Toward the stair where a pageant unfurled,
To reveal to their view, dancing down, two by two,
    The most beautiful girls in the world.

And as Nebulous stared, he gave thanks he'd been spared:
    "Praise to all of the gods who protect us!"
For, with shuffles and twirls, dancing down with the girls,
    There was Phallus Toujourus Erectus.

"All I needed to do to make him come to you,"
    Called his chum as they passed in review,
"Was to pay the girls' fee to have them follow me,
    Knowing Phallus would come along too."

LeRoy Carl Blake

Then, as if on some cue from a god, out of view,
    There appeared in the midst of the show
Grievous' wife, to one side, with Fair Ampla, the bride,
    And a phalanx of servants in tow.

Thus, with those saving graces set firm in their places,
    The bard bent once more to the ear
Of Vexatious, who'd said he would see Phallus dead,
    And he made himself perfectly clear:

"If you kill him, I swear your son won't have a prayer
    Against Flatula, who will prevail,
But if you will forgive, and allow him to live,
    I'll swear likewise to you that she'll fail!

"For the Celt had to vow, just as you did, just now,
    To an unnamed 'condition' I made,
Which is: Now he must pay for his fun yesterday
    Or be skewered alive on your blade.

"Now, his payment should be – and I'm sure you'll agree –
    To ensure his complete restitution,
That he take for a wife – thereby saving his life –
    Fragrant Flatula, queen of pollution."

NEBULOUS IN LOVE

But as Nebulous spoke he heard somebody choke,
    And he turned to hear Phallus explode:
"There is no way in *Hell* I will marry the belle
    With the smell of an open commode!"

"Ah, but Phallus, my friend, I would fain recommend
    That you take a more positive view,"
Softly Nebulous said with a nod of his head
    Toward Vexatious, who picked up his cue:

"The boy's right, for a change, though I do find it strange
    To agree with the Ludicrous wit:
You *will* marry the belle of the singular smell,
    Or you'll bleed like a pig on a spit!"

"Well, of course I just may, since you put it that way,
    Find that marriage is quite to my taste,"
Stammered Phallus, in fear for the life he held dear,
    "But with Flatula I'd be disgraced!"

"What's a little disgrace if it serves to displace
    Your new rank as a load of dead meat?"
Prodded Nebulous, who hinted saying "I do"
    Was how Phallus could land on his feet.

"Yes, I do take your point," said the Celt, out of joint
      Between loathing and fear for his life,
"May I state at this time I would deem it *sublime*
      To take Sleazum's – ugh! – daughter to wife."

"I'll be damned if you will!" shouted Sleazum, who still
      Was in earshot of all that was said.
"No one here shall command who'll win Flatula's hand
      Except *me* and I *know* whom she'll wed."

"As a man of your word," gently Nebulous purred,
      "Surely you must recall that you said,
'If his wealth and his name are as great or the same,
      I'll consider another instead?'

"Well, the 'other' is here in the guise of our dear
      (Though misjudged, it would seem) Gallic friend,
Whose estates and whose fame make Vexatious look lame,
      And whom *I*, my good man, recommend.

"So instead of a sneer, spread a smile of good cheer
      And rejoice in the scope of your coup,
Because Phallus, the fop, has good friends at the top,
      Which means you'll be connected there too."

NEBULOUS IN LOVE

While his eyes held a gleam as his transparent dream
    Of ambition became crystal clear,
The old merchant hissed, "*Done!* Welcome, Phallus, my son!"
    But the Celt was too heartsick to hear.

Now, Coita got bored when she wasn't adored
    Or receiving a lecherous pat,
So the Hunk's manly chest and his boilerplate vest
    Drew her over to strike up a chat.

Leaving Nebulous' side like a phantom, to glide
    Into orbit around her new stud,
She observed with a smile how her feminine wile
    Could so easily heat a man's blood.

And the look that Hunk gave in return sent a wave
    Through his friends and detractors combined
That bespoke his intent to vouchsafe his assent
    To whatever she had on her mind.

"I'm so glad you approve of Coita's first move,"
    Offered Nebulous, flashing a grin;
Though his smile, past the nose that spread out like a rose
    Was misshapen and woefully thin.

LeRoy Carl Blake

"Because now I am sure you'll be happy with her
      Through the years on your journey ahead
As you walk, man and wife, down the highway of life
      Filled with gladness and love when you've wed.

"And you'll add to your fame when this tramp takes your name,
      For Vexatious will join with your dad
In ensuring that you get the rank that you're due
      In the place of the rank that you had."

"And would you care to bet on the help he will get,"
      Growled Vexatious, "from little old *me*,
Since your stupid 'condition' confirms Hunk's position
      As son-in-law never-to-be?"

"Now, don't tell me I've erred in assuming you cared,
      Good Vexatious! How soon you forget
That while Hunkus is free Ampla can't marry me,
      For she's promised to him, I regret.

"But if Hunkus were wed to Coita instead,
      In exchange for a General's rank,
Then your daughter and I would be free to ally
      In a marriage, and have you to thank.

NEBULOUS IN LOVE

"But, if you'd rather not help the Hunk get his shot
    At commanding a legion of men,
I'll release Phallus now from his unholy vow,
    Setting Flatula free once again."

Gorgeosus' jaw dropped and his heart almost stopped
    And he yawped, "What is this you impart?
Did you say that my boy, my own pride and true joy,
    Should be married to that little *tart*?

"Who the hell are *you*, then, that you peddle these men
    As if they were mere straws in a game
To be drawn, without voice, by a spouse of *your* choice
    Who enjoys neither wealth nor good name?

"My agreement is clear! Hunkus weds Ampla dear,
    Not a strumpet from some catacomb;
He would just get the rap, not to mention the clap,
    For the biggest class come-down in Rome.

"And what's more, I'm afraid, no 'condition' was made
    Between me *or* my Hunkus and you
Like the one with the Gaul and Vexatious withal,
    So buzz off with your who-marries-who!"

LeRoy Carl Blake

Pouted Nebulous, "Then I have erred yet *again*?
    I was sure you'd be tickled to tears
That your son could now bank on the General's rank
    That you swore he's had coming for years.

"For the Senate, of course, is the living god's source
    For recruiting brave men for that rank,
And he's swayed by the word – never mind how absurd –
    Of Vexatious, the head mountebank.

"Oh, and last but not least: If you think you've been fleeced
    And your pact with Vexatious is dead,
You'll be happy to hear that your daughter made clear
    That Pragmaticus asked her to wed."

But when Hunkus, who'd heard ev'ry troth-swapping word,
    Said it just wasn't his cup of tea,
Gorgeosus said, "Hunk, put a sock in it, punk!
    Whom you'll marry is still up to me!"

And so Nebulous thought, *the good fight has been fought!*
    In the end I proved love conquers all –
Though they all called me wrong, I was right all along!
    And he felt he was ten cubits tall.

NEBULOUS IN LOVE

But his pleasure soon fled, for Vexatious then said,
    "Look at *me*! *I'm* the only one present
Who is not better set than at noon when we met,
    And especially that wine-peddling peasant!

"See Emporium, there, with his new, haughty air
    After hitching his odious whelp
To our former old friend who in turn must extend
    To the merchant his pedigreed help,

"And see Hunkus, who, now that he's broken his vow
    To my daughter, may wed whom he will,
And as part of our thanks, he gets named to the ranks
    For which most other soldiers would kill.

"Gorgeosus, you, too, have been tried and found true
    To the side which can make the best deal:
Such unwavering trust in fidelity must
    Be the way you became such a wheel!

"Even Phallus – you jerk! – found a noteworthy perk,
    To wit: Marriage is good for his health;
And the odds, I confess, are quite good for success
    (But they change if he loses his wealth).

LeRoy Carl Blake

"But *my* prize for today was snatched boldly away
    By the lad who has stolen my dower:
I mean Nebulous, who, after all's said and through,
    Stole my daughter through raw, naked power."

And the gathering crowd began grumbling aloud
    As Vexatious kept leading them on,
When a voice from his rear caught the Senator's ear,
    Saying, "*Whom* are you trying to con?"

Every head spun around toward the magistral sound –
    Grim Vexatious' words died on his lips –
To observe, standing there in the afternoon glare,
    Hideosa, her hands on her hips.

"If you're lost for a name to connect with the blame
    For the fact that you've just been outclassed,
Take a look in the pool at the face of the fool
    Who got caught with his drawers at half-mast.

"*You're* the arrogant ass who brought all this to pass
    From your personal Pandora's box
When you tried playing house with the Emperor's spouse
    Wearing nothing but sandals and socks.

NEBULOUS IN LOVE

"Let the facts become known! This young lad, on his own,
      Came across when it came to the crunch;
He has salvaged your bum *and* Pragmaticus from
      Watching Sleazum, the scum, eat your lunch.

"Now, I add further gain (Though it gives me a pain)
      To your overblown, lofty repute,
For I, too, made a hedge that, should Coita pledge
      To be wed, I would follow her suit.

"And since Hunkus is doomed Oops! I mean, it's *assumed*
      That he'll marry my sister today,
I have given my hand, as young Nebulous planned,
      To his father, who swept me away.

"Which, Vexatious, old man, means I'm joining the clan
      Of the blue blooded Ludicrous name,
Making Nebulous *rich*, and thus worthy to hitch
      Any girl who conforms to the same."

As the message sank in through his leathery skin,
      And a smile drew the veil from his joy,
The old Senator crooned, his demeanor re-tuned,
      "Honored Nebulous! Welcome, my boy!"

LeRoy Carl Blake

But the eloquent word which the solon preferred
    To a substantive statement of fact
Died adrift on the air, for the crowd ceased to care
    When Vexatious went into his act.

And the ones that he chose to most savor his prose
    (All the blue-bloods and Sleazum, *per se*)
Had, when Spectra was done, moved apart, as if one,
    And began slowly walking away.

Spectra strolled arm in arm oozing radiant charm
    With old Virtuous Ludicrous, who,
Safely saved from his straits, thanked the Sisterly Fates
    For their favor in seeing him through;

And Pragmaticus, too, whose own dream had come true
    In the form of Delicia, the "dish,"
Walked a pace or two after young Hunkus, whose laughter
    Was all that Coita could wish.

It was only the Celt, for whom nobody felt
    Any pity for what he had done,
Who trudged glumly apart with a tear in his heart
    For the poor, wretched maid he had won.

NEBULOUS IN LOVE

In the midst of the group, like a king with his troop,
    Happy Nebulous glided on air,
With the girl at his side for whom he would have died
    Had his dying but made them a pair.

And now, lovers at last, tasting joy unsurpassed
    And set free from the day's heavy cares,
They both fled from the din at Juturna's old inn
    In a dash up the Palatine Stairs.

"Spectra knew from the start I had won the true heart,
    Shouted Nebulous, giddy with life,
"Of the damsel I love, in conclusion whereof
    she and I will become man and wife!"

When they reached the first stop on their way to the top,
    Happy Nebulous turned to his love,
And with arms opened wide he enclosed her inside,
    Like a tenderly snug-fitting glove.

Then they rose, hearts aglow, up that stair long ago
    On the breath of a spring afternoon,
Pledging love with their eyes beneath Rome's azure skies
    On the nones of a halcyon June.

LeRoy Carl Blake

And, as they drift away on this lovely June day,
      Toward The Hill from the Forum of Rome,
Tripping lightly on air in their world without care,
      We must also be heading for home.

For we've come to the end of our journey, my friend,
      And the tale that I wanted to tell;
We will meet once again when I've new tales to pen –
      Until then, my *amicus* . . . Farewell.

THE END

GLOSSARY

Atrium:	The central, open courtyard of a Roman house
Aureas:	A Roman gold coin
Bark:	A type of three-masted sailing vessel
Calends:	The first day of the Roman month
Calliope:	The Muse of Eloquence and Epic Poetry
Canaille:	The rabble; a low-born person
Carcer:	A jail or prison
Carnis Mortuus:	Dead meat
Celt:	The Celt: A reference to Phallus Toujourus Erectus
Ceres:	The Roman Goddess of Grain and Harvests
Cubiculum:	A cubicle (a small room); a bedroom
Curia:	The Roman Senate House
Dewlap:	The pendulous skin under the chin of an old person
Dignitas:	Personal dignity, authority, rank, reputation
Erato:	The Muse of Lyric and Love Poetry

Gaul:	1) The region roughly equivalent to modern France
	2) The Gaul: A reference to Phallus Toujourus Erectus
Gaul Cisalpina:	The Roman side of the Alps; site of present day Milan
Hecate's Daughter:	The goddess Circe, best known for turning Odysseus's crew into swine
Hoi Polloi	The citizenry; the people; the bourgeoisie; the lower middle class, etc. (Gk.)
Holy of Holies:	A reference to Phallus's tablinum
Ides:	The fifteenth day of March, June, July, and October; the thirteenth day of the other months
Juturna	The Roman Goddess of Springs
Libra:	A pound; *A ten-libra bag of cement*
Minerva:	Pallas Athena to the Greeks, Minerva was the Roman Goddess of War or Battle
Nones:	The fifth day of all the months except March, May, July, and October
Parvenu:	An upstart
Paterfamilias:	The head of a Roman household; a patriarch
Peristyle:	A system of columns lining an inner courtyard; an entrance way
Pet:	A fit of pique or ill temper

NEBULOUS IN LOVE

Praefectus:	A Prefect; a Governor; a Commander
Proximus Locus:	The next place, next location
Scion:	A descendant; an heir
Snickersnee:	A dagger
Solon:	A Senator
Sturm & Drang:	Stress & strain
Tablinum:	An internal, private room reserved for family use; The study of the Paterfamilias
Tarpeian Rock:	The cliff from which condemned persons were thrown; a place of execution
Thalia:	The Muse of Comedy and Pastoral Poetry
Triclinium:	The dining room in a Roman house; a dining couch
The Weird Three:	The Fates
Togated:	To be dressed in a toga
Togated Wonder:	A reference to Grievous Vexatious